CHICAGO
RODEN
6083 NORTHWEST HGWY
P9-DKF-479
APR - - 2009
DISCARD

PUFFIN CLASSICS

Aladdin and Other Tales from the Arabian Nights

The Tales from the Arabian Nights (also known as *The Thousand and One Nights*) have been popular in the West ever since they were first introduced at the beginning of the eighteenth century. There have been many different versions in print, pantomime and on film, but here they are retold directly from the authentic Arabic sources.

Collected together in this edition are some of the best-known stories, such as *Aladdin* and *The Ebony Horse*, as well as the lesser-known *Khalifah the Fisherman* and *The Dream*. The stories, which originate from Persia, India and Arabia, were the daily entertainment of ordinary people. In this edition they are presented in a way that is straightforward but not over-simplified, so that they are as fresh and as vivid as they were when first told over a thousand years ago.

Born in Baghdad, N. J. DAWOOD went to England as an Iraq State Scholar in 1945 and graduated from London University. In 1959 he founded the Arabic Advertising and Publishing Company, London, which is now one of the major centres for Arabic typesetting outside the Middle East. He translated *The Koran* and an unexpurgated collection of *Tales from the Thousand and One Nights* and edited and abridged *The Muqaddimah of Ibn Khaldun*. Mr Dawood has also translated numerous technical works into Arabic, written and spoken radio and film commentaries, and contributed to specialized English–Arabic dictionaries.

The illustrations are from the famous original engravings on wood made by William Harvey in 1839.

Some other Puffin Classics to enjoy

SINBAD THE SAILOR AND OTHER TALES
N. J. Dawood

THE WIZARD OF OZ
L. Frank Baum

ALICE'S ADVENTURES IN WONDERLAND
THROUGH THE LOOKING GLASS
Lewis Carroll

THE CANTERBURY TALES
Geoffrey Chaucer
Retold by Geraldine McCaughrean

THE ADVENTURES OF ROBIN HOOD
TALES OF GREEK HEROES
Roger Lancelyn Green

THE RIME OF THE ANCIENT MARINER
AND OTHER CLASSIC STORIES IN VERSE
Roger Waterfield (Ed.)

THE HAPPY PRINCE AND OTHER STORIES
Oscar Wilde

N. J. DAWOOD

Aladdin and Other Tales from the Arabian Nights

Retold from the Original Arabic

Engravings on wood from original designs by

WILLIAM HARVEY

PUFFIN BOOKS

To Juliet, Richard, Norman, and Andrew

This version follows Macnaghten's Calcutta edition of *The Thousand and One Nights* (1839–42) but the first Bulaq edition (1835) has also been consulted wherever the Macnaghten text appeared faulty. 'Aladdin and the Enchanted Lamp' follows Zottenberg's text (Paris, 1888).

PUFFIN BOOKS

Published by the Penguin Group
Penguin Books Ltd, 80 Strand, London WC2R 0RL, England
Penguin Putnam Inc., 375 Hudson Street, New York, New York 10014, USA
Penguin Books Australia Ltd, 250 Camberwell Road, Camberwell, Victoria 3124, Australia
Penguin Books Canada Ltd, 10 Alcorn Avenue, Toronto, Ontario, Canada M4V 3B2
Penguin Books India (P) Ltd, 11 Community Centre, Panchsheel Park, New Delhi – 110 017, India
Penguin Books (NZ) Ltd, Cnr Rosedale and Airborne Roads, Albany, Auckland, New Zealand
Penguin Books (South Africa) (Pty) Ltd, 24 Sturdee Avenue, Rosebank 2196, South Africa

Penguin Books Ltd, Registered Offices: 80 Strand, London WC2R 0RL, England

www.penguin.com

This translation first published in the USA by Doubleday & Company, Inc. 1978
Published in Puffin Books 1989
Reissued in this edition 1996
22

This translation copyright © N. J. Dawood, 1978
All rights reserved

Filmset by Datix International Limited, Bungay, Suffolk
Printed in the UK by CPI Bookmarque, Croydon, CR0 4TD
Set 12/15 pt Monophoto Plantin

Except in the United States of America, this book is sold subject to the condition that it shall not, by way of trade or otherwise, be lent, re-sold, hired out, or otherwise circulated without the publisher's prior consent in any form of binding or cover other than that in which it is published and without a similar condition including this condition being imposed on the subsequent purchaser

ISBN: 978-0-14036-782-9

R0420974362

CHICAGO PUBLIC LIBRARY
RODEN BRANCH
6083 NORTHWEST HGWY. 60631

Contents

Prologue

The Tale of King Shahriyar and His Brother, Shahzaman

Once upon a time, there ruled over India and China a mighty King, who commanded great armies and had numerous courtiers, followers, and servants. He left two sons, both famed for their horsemanship – especially the elder, who inherited his father's kingdom and governed it with such justice that all his subjects loved him. He was called King Shahriyar. His brother was named Shahzaman and was King of Samarkand.

The two brothers continued to reign happily in their kingdoms, and after twenty years King Shahriyar longed to see Shahzaman. He ordered his vizier to go to Samarkand and invite Shahzaman to his court.

The vizier set out promptly on his errand and journeyed many days and nights through deserts and wildernesses until he arrived in Shahzaman's city and was admitted to his presence. He gave him King Shahriyar's greetings and told him of his master's wish to see him. King Shahzaman was overjoyed at the thought of visiting his brother. He made ready to leave his kingdom, and sent out his tents, camels, mules, servants, and retainers. Then he appointed his vizier as his deputy and set out for his brother's dominions.

At midnight, however, he suddenly remembered a present which he wished to give his brother but which he had left at the palace. He returned alone to fetch it. Entering his private chamber, he was outraged to find his beautiful queen, whose affection he had never doubted, entertaining a palace slave.

'If this can happen when I am scarcely out of my city,' he thought, 'what will this wicked woman do when I am far away?'

He drew his sword and slew them both. Then he rejoined his courtiers and journeyed on until he reached his brother's capital.

Shahriyar rejoiced at his coming. He went out to meet Shahzaman, took him in his arms, and welcomed him affectionately. But as they sat chatting, he noticed that Shahzaman, who was brooding over his wife's disloyalty, looked pale and sullen. Shahriyar said nothing about this, thinking that his brother might be worrying over the affairs of the kingdom he had left behind. Day after day Shahriyar tried to distract him, but all to no avail. At last he invited him to go hunting, hoping that the sport might cheer his spirits, but Shahzaman refused, and Shahriyar had to go to the hunt alone.

Meanwhile, Shahzaman sat at a window overlooking the royal garden, and saw one of the palace doors open and twenty women and twenty slaves appear. In their midst was his brother's Queen, a woman of rare beauty. They made their way to the fountain and sat down on the grass, each slave choosing a woman for his companion. Then the King's wife called out, 'Come, Masood!' and a slave at once ran up to her and sat down beside her. There they all remained, feasting together, till nightfall.

'By Allah,' said Shahzaman to himself, 'my misfortune was nothing beside this.'

He was no longer unhappy, but ate and drank, being hungry after his long abstinence.

When Shahriyar returned from the hunt he was surprised to see his brother restored to health and good spirits.

'How is it, brother,' he asked, 'that when I last saw you, you were so pale and sad, and now you look well and contented?'

'As for my sadness,' Shahzaman replied, 'I will now tell you the reason. Know that after I had received your invitation I made preparations for the journey and set out from my capital; but I had forgotten the pearl that was my present for you, and went back to the palace for it. There in my room I found my wife in the company of a slave. I killed them both. Then I came on to your kingdom, though my mind was troubled with unhappy thoughts.'

When he heard this, Shahriyar was curious to know the rest of the story, upon which Shahzaman related to him all that he had seen that day from the window.

'I will not believe it,' Shahriyar exclaimed, 'unless I see it with my own eyes!'

'Then let it be known that you intend to hunt again,' suggested his brother. 'But hide with me here, and you will see what I saw.'

And so King Shahriyar announced his intention to set out on another expedition. Soldiers, with their tents, left the city, and Shahriyar followed them. As soon as they had encamped, he gave orders to his slaves that no one was to be admitted to the King's tent. Then, disguising himself, he returned unnoticed to the palace, where his brother was waiting for him. They sat together at one of the windows overlooking the garden. It was not long before the Queen and her women appeared with the slaves and thus King Shahriyar saw that what his brother had told him was true.

Crazed with anger, he put his Queen to death, together with all her women and the slaves. And after that he made it his custom to marry a young girl every day and kill her the next morning. This he continued to do for three years, until an outcry arose among the people, and some of them left the country with their daughters.

At last a day came when the King's vizier searched the city in vain for a wife for his master. Finding none, and dreading the King's anger, he returned home with a heavy heart.

Now, the vizier himself had two daughters. The

older was called Shahrazad, and the younger Dunyazad. Shahrazad was both beautiful and accomplished: she knew the works of poets and the legends of ancient kings.

Shahrazad noticed her father's anxiety and asked what made him so sad. The vizier told her the reason. 'Dear Father,' she said, 'give me in marriage to the King. Either I will die a martyr's death, or I will live and save my countrymen's daughters.'

Her proposal filled the vizier with horror. He warned her how dangerous it would be; but she had made up her mind and would not listen to his advice.

'Beware,' said the vizier, 'of what happened in the fable of the donkey who did not mind his own business.'

The Fable of the Donkey, the Ox, and the Farmer

There was once a rich farmer who owned many herds of cattle. He understood the language of beasts and birds. In one of his stables he kept an ox and a donkey. At the end of each day the ox came to where the donkey was tied and found the stall well swept and watered. The manger was plentifully supplied with straw and barley, and the donkey lying at his ease, for his master seldom rode him.

It happened one day that the farmer heard the ox say to the donkey, 'How lucky you are! I am worn out with hard work, but you lie here in comfort. The corn you eat is well prepared and you lack nothing. Our master hardly ever rides you. But for me life is one long stretch of painful labor at the plow and the millstone.'

The donkey answered, 'Let me advise you. When you go out into the field and the yoke is placed upon your neck, pretend to be ill and drop down on your belly. Do not rise even if they beat you; or, if you do rise, fall down again immediately. When they take you back to the stable and put fodder before you, do not eat it. For a day or two eat very little. If you act in this way you will be given a complete rest.'

Remember, the farmer overheard this.

So when the plowman brought his fodder, the ox ate hardly any of it. And when the plowman came the following morning to take him out into the field the ox appeared to be far from well. The farmer said, 'Take the donkey and use him at the plow all day!'

The day's work being finished, the donkey returned to the stable. The ox thanked him for his kind advice, but the donkey made no reply, bitterly repenting his rashness.

Next day the plowman took the donkey again and made him labor until the evening, so that he returned utterly exhausted, with his neck chafed by the rope. Again the ox thanked him and complimented him on his shrewdness.

'I wish I had kept my wisdom to myself,' thought the donkey.

Then an idea came to him.

Turning to the ox, he said, 'I heard my master say to his servant just now, "If the ox does not recover soon, take him to the slaughterhouse and get rid of him." My fear for your safety, dear friend, obliges me to make this known to you before it is too late.'

On hearing the donkey's words, the ox thanked him and said, 'Tomorrow I will work willingly.' He ate all his fodder and even licked the manger clean.

Early the next morning the farmer went with his wife to visit the ox in the stable. At the sight of his master the ox swung his tail and frisked about in all directions to show how ready he was for the yoke. He was taken to work by the plowman. And so was the donkey.

'Nothing will change my mind, Father,' Shahrazad said at the end of the story. 'I am resolved.'

So the vizier arrayed his daughter in bridal garments, decked her with jewels, and made ready to announce her wedding to the King.

When she said good-by to her sister, Shahrazad gave her these instructions: 'After I have been received by the King I shall send for you. When you come, you must say, "Tell us, sister, some tale of marvel to pass the night." Then I will tell you a tale which, if Allah wills, shall be the means of our deliverance.'

So the vizier went with his daughter to the

King. And when the King had taken Shahrazad to his chamber she wept and said, 'I have a young sister to whom I dearly wish to say a last farewell.'

The King sent for Dunyazad, who came and threw her arms around her sister's neck and sat down beside her.

Then Dunyazad said to Shahrazad, 'Tell us, sister, a tale of marvel so that the night may pass pleasantly.'

'Gladly,' she answered, 'if the King permits me.'

The King, who was troubled with sleeplessness, gave her leave and eagerly listened to Shahrazad's story:

The Fisherman and the Jinnee

Once upon a time, there was a poor fisherman who had a wife and three children to support.

He used to cast his net four times a day. It chanced that one day he went down to the sea at noon and, reaching the shore, set down his basket, rolled up his sleeves, and cast his net far out into the water. After he had waited for some time, he pulled on the cords with all his strength, but the net was so heavy that he could not draw it in. So he tied the rope ends to a wooden stake on the beach, took off his clothes, dived into the water, and set to work to bring up the net. But when he had carried it ashore he found that it contained only a dead donkey. 'What a strange catch!' cried the fisherman, disgusted at the sight. He freed the net and wrung it out, then waded into the water and cast it again. On trying to draw it in, he found it even heavier than before. Thinking he had caught some enormous fish, he fastened the ropes to the stake, dived in again, and brought up the net. This time he found a large earthen vessel filled with mud and sand.

Angrily the fisherman threw away the vessel, cleaned his net, and cast it for the third time. He waited patiently and, when he felt the net grow heavy, pulled it in, only to find it full of bones and broken glass. In despair, he lifted up his arms and cried, 'Heaven knows I cast my net only four times a day. I have already cast it for the third time and caught no fish at all. Surely Allah will not fail me again!'

So saying, the fisherman hurled his net far out into the sea. This time his catch was an antique bottle made of copper. The mouth was stopped with lead and bore the seal of King Solomon, who was renowned for his great skill in magic and his power over spirits and demons. The fisherman rejoiced and said, 'I will sell this in the market of the coppersmiths. It must be worth ten pieces of gold.'

Shaking the bottle, which he found rather heavy, he thought, 'I must break the seal and see what there is inside.'

With his knife he removed the lead and again shook the bottle; but scarcely had he done so when there burst out from it a great column of smoke that spread along the shore and rose so high that it almost touched the heavens. Then the smoke took shape and formed itself into a jinnee of such colossal height that his head touched the clouds. His legs towered like the masts of a ship. His head was a huge dome and his mouth as wide as a cavern, with teeth ragged as broken rocks. His nostrils were two inverted bowls, and his eyes, blazing like torches, made his face terrible indeed to look upon.

The sight of the jinnee struck fear into the fisherman's heart; his limbs trembled, his teeth chattered, his tongue dried, and his eyes bulged.

'There is no god but Allah, and Solomon is his Prophet!' cried the jinnee, taking the fisherman for the magician-king, his old master. 'I beg you, mighty prophet, do not kill me! I swear never again to disobey you.'

'What on earth are you talking about?' the fisherman cried. 'Solomon has been dead these eighteen hundred years, and we are now nearing the end of time. But what is your story, and how did you come to be imprisoned in this bottle?'

The jinnee seemed very pleased to hear that Solomon was dead. He burst out laughing, then said sarcastically, 'Fisherman, rejoice. I bring you good news!'

'What news?'

'News of your death, horrible and instant!' the jinnee answered.

'Ungrateful wretch!' the fisherman cried. 'Why do you wish my death? What have I done to deserve it? Have I not brought you up from the depths of the sea and released you from your imprisonment?'

But the jinnee commanded, 'Choose the manner of your death and the way that I shall kill you. Come, waste no time!'

'But how have I wronged you?'

'Listen to my story, and you will know the reason,' the jinnee answered.

'Be brief, then, I beg you,' the fisherman pleaded, 'for you have wrung my soul with fear.'

'Know,' the giant began, 'that I am one of the rebel demons who rose up in arms against King Solomon. The King sent to me his commander in chief, who captured me, despite my power, and led me in fetters before his master. Invoking the name of God, Solomon ordered me to embrace his faith and pledge him absolute obedience. I refused, and he imprisoned me in this bottle, and set upon it a seal of lead bearing the name of the Most High. Then he sent for several of his faithful demons, who carried me away and cast me into the middle of the sea. In the ocean depths I vowed, "I will bestow eternal riches on him who sets me free!" But a hundred years passed away and no one freed me. In the second hundred years of my imprisonment I said, "For him who frees me I will open up the buried treasures of the earth!" And yet no one freed me. Whereupon I flew into a rage and swore, "I will kill the man who sets me free, allowing him only to choose the manner of his death!" Now it was you who set me free; therefore prepare to die and choose the way that I shall kill you.'

'Oh, wretched luck, that I should be the one to free you!' the fisherman exclaimed. 'Spare me, mighty jinnee, and Allah will spare you; kill me, and so will Allah destroy you!'

'You have freed me,' said the jinnee; 'therefore you must die.'

'Noble jinnee, will you repay good with evil?'

'Enough of this babble! Kill you I must.'

At this point the fisherman thought to himself, 'Though I am only a helpless human being and he is a powerful jinnee, I may yet have sense enough to outwit him.' To the monster he said, 'Before you kill me, I beg you in the Name of the Most High, engraved on Solomon's seal, to answer me one question truthfully.'

The jinnee trembled at the mention of the Name, and, when he had promised to answer truthfully, the fisherman asked, 'How could this bottle, which is scarcely big enough to hold your hand or foot, ever contain your entire body?'

'Do you doubt that?' the jinnee roared indignantly.

'I will never believe it,' the fisherman replied, 'until I have seen you enter this bottle with my own eyes.'

Upon this the jinnee shook from head to foot and dissolved into a column of smoke, which gradually wound itself into the bottle and disappeared within. At once the fisherman snatched up the leaden stopper and thrust it into the mouth of the vessel. Then he called out to the jinnee, 'Now you must choose the manner of your death and the way that I shall kill you. Upon my life, I will throw you back into the sea, and warn all men against your treachery!'

When he heard the fisherman's words, the jinnee struggled hard to get out, but the magic seal held him back. He now altered his tone and, assuming a humble air, said that he had been jesting, and begged to be freed. But the fisherman paid no attention to his cries and took the bottle down to the seashore.

'What are you going to do with me?' whimpered the jinnee.

'I am going to throw you back into the sea!' the fisherman replied. 'You have lain in the depths for eighteen hundred years, and there you shall remain till the Last Judgment! Did I not beg you to spare me so that Allah might spare you? But you took no pity on me, and he has now delivered you into my hands.'

'Let me out,' the jinnee begged, 'and I will give you fabulous riches!'

'Faithless jinnee,' the fisherman answered, 'you deserve no better fate than that of the King in the tale of Yunan and the doctor.'

'What tale is that?' asked the jinnee.

The Tale of King Yunan and Duban the Doctor

It is said (the fisherman began) that once upon a time there reigned in the land of Persia a rich and mighty King called Yunan. He had great armies and a numerous following of noblemen and courtiers. But he suffered from a leprosy that his physicians, for all their skill and knowledge, could never cure.

One day a venerable old doctor named Duban came to the King's capital. He had studied books written in Greek, Latin, Arabic, and Persian and was deeply read in the lore of the ancients. He was master of many sciences, knew the properties of plants and herbs, and, above all, was skilled in astrology and medicine. When this physician heard of the King's leprosy and of his doctors' vain attempts to cure him, he put on his finest robes and went off to the royal palace. After he had kissed the ground before the King and invoked blessings upon him, he told him who he was and said, 'Great King, I have heard about your illness and have come to heal you. Yet will I give you no medicine to drink, nor any ointment to rub upon your body.'

The King was astonished at the doctor's words.

'How will you do that?' he asked. 'If you cure me, I will heap riches upon you, and your children's children after you. Anything you wish shall be yours for the asking, and you shall be my companion and friend. But when is it to be? What day, what hour?'

'Tomorrow, if the King wishes,' came the reply.

The King gave Duban a robe of honor and other presents, and the doctor took leave of him. Hastening to the center of the town, he rented a little house to which he carried his books and his drugs and other medicaments. Then he prepared the cure and poured it into a hollow polo stick.

Next morning Duban went to the royal palace, kissed the ground before the King, and asked him to ride into the field and play a game of polo with his friends. The King rode out with his ministers and his chamberlains, and when he had entered the playing field the doctor handed him the hollow club and said, 'Take this and grasp it firmly. Strike the ball with all your might until the palm of your hand and the rest of your body begin to sweat. The cure will penetrate your palm and run through your veins and arteries. When it has done its work, return to the palace, wash yourself, and go to sleep. In this way you will be cured; and peace be with you.'

The King took hold of the club and, gripping it firmly, struck the ball and galloped after it with the other players. Harder and harder he hit the ball as he dashed up and down the field, until his palm and his body perspired.

Duban saw that the cure was working, and he ordered the King to return to the palace. The slaves hastened to make ready the royal bath and to prepare the linens and the towels. The King bathed, put on his night clothes, and went to sleep.

Next morning the physician went to the palace. When he was admitted to the King's presence he kissed the ground before him and wished him peace. The King quickly got up to receive him, threw his arms around the physician's neck, and seated him by his side.

For when the King had left his bath the previous evening, he had looked upon his body and rejoiced to find no trace of the leprosy; his skin had become as pure as virgin silver. And so the King entertained the physician liberally again all the day. He also bestowed on him robes of honor and other gifts and, when evening came, gave him two thousand pieces of gold and mounted him on his own favorite horse. So thrilled was the King at the extraordinary skill of his doctor that he kept repeating to himself, 'This wise physician has cured me without drug or ointment. By Allah, I will load him with honors and make him my companion and trusted friend.' And that night the King lay down to sleep in an ecstasy of bliss, knowing that he was clean in body and cured of his disease.

Next day, as soon as he was seated upon his throne, with the officers of his court standing before him and his lieutenants and ministers on either side, the King called for the physician, who came up and kissed the ground before him. The King rose and seated the doctor by his side. He feasted him all day, gave him a thousand pieces of gold and more robes of honor, and talked with him until nightfall.

Now, among the King's viziers was a wicked old man, an envious, spiteful villain. Seeing the King make the physician his favorite friend and lavish on him high dignities and favors, the vizier began to plot the doctor's ruin. So, on the following day, when the King entered the council chamber and was about to call for the physician, the vizier kissed the ground before him and said, 'Your Majesty, my duty prompts me to warn you against an evil that threatens your life; nor would I be anything but a traitor if I held my peace.'

Troubled at these ominous words, the King ordered him to explain what he meant.

'Your Majesty,' the vizier went on, 'there is an old proverb that says: "He who does not weigh the consequences of his acts will never prosper." Now, I have seen the King bestow favors and shower honors upon his enemy, a murderer who is secretly plotting to destroy him. I greatly fear for the King's safety.'

'Who is this man whom you suppose to be my enemy?' asked the King, turning pale.

'I speak of Duban the doctor,' the vizier answered.

'He is my friend,' replied the King angrily, 'dearer to me than all my courtiers; for he has cured me of my leprosy, an evil that my own physicians could not remove. Surely there is no other man like him in the whole world, from East to West. How can you say these monstrous things of him? From this day I will appoint him my personal doctor, and give him every month a thousand pieces of gold. Even if I gave him half my kingdom, it would be only a trifling payment for his service. Your advice, my vizier, is born of jealousy and envy. Would you have me kill my savior and repent of my rashness, as the King in the story repented after he had killed his falcon?'

The Tale of the King and the Falcon

Once upon a time (King Yunan went on), there was a Persian King who was a great lover of riding and hunting. He had a falcon which he himself had trained with loving care and which never left his side for a moment. Even at night-time he carried it perched upon his wrist, and when he went hunting he took it with him. Hanging from the bird's neck was a golden bowl from which it drank. One day the King ordered his men to make ready for a hunting expedition and, taking his falcon with him, rode out with his courtiers. At last they came to a valley where they laid the hunting nets. A gazelle fell into the snare, and the King said, 'I will kill the man who lets her escape!'

They drew the nets closer and closer around the animal. On seeing the King, the gazelle stood on her haunches and raised her forelegs to her head as if she wished to salute him. But as he bent forward to lay hold of her she leaped over his head and fled across the field. Looking around, the King saw his courtiers winking at one another.

'Why are they winking?' he asked his vizier.

'Perhaps because you let the beast escape,' answered the other, smiling.

'On my life,' cried the King, 'I will chase this gazelle and bring her back!'

At once he galloped off in pursuit of the fleeing animal. When he had caught up with her, his falcon swooped upon the gazelle, and the King struck her down with a blow of his sword. Then he dismounted and hung the carcass on his saddle-bow.

It was a hot day and the King, who by this time had become faint with thirst, went to search for water. Presently he saw a huge tree, down whose trunk water was trickling in great drops. He took the little bowl from the falcon's neck, filled it up, and placed it before the bird. But the falcon knocked the bowl with its beak and tipped it over. The King once again filled the bowl and placed it before the falcon, but the bird knocked it over a second time. At this the King became very angry; he filled the bowl a third time and set it before his horse. But the falcon sprang forward and knocked it over with its wings.

'Vile creature!' the King exclaimed. 'You have prevented yourself from drinking, and the horse too.'

So saying, he struck the falcon with his sword and cut off both its wings. But the bird lifted its head as if to say, 'Look into the tree!' The King raised his eyes and saw an enormous serpent spitting its poison down the trunk.

The King was deeply sorry for his action. Mounting his horse, he hurried back to the palace. No sooner had he sat down, with the falcon still perched on his wrist, than the bird gave a violent gasp and dropped down dead.

The King was stricken with sorrow and remorse for killing the bird that had saved his life.

When the vizier heard King Yunan's story he said, 'I assure Your Majesty that my only concern is for your safety. I beg leave to warn you that if you put your trust in this physician, it is certain that he will destroy you. Did he not cure you by a device held in the hand? And might he not cause your death by another such device?'

This convinced the King. 'You have spoken wisely, my faithful vizier. Indeed, it is quite probable that this physician has come to my court as a spy to destroy me. And since he cured my illness by a thing held in the hand, he might as cleverly poison me with something different, such as the scent of a perfume. What should I do, my vizier?'

'Send for him at once, and when he comes, strike off his head. Only in this way will you be safe from his designs.'

Thereupon the King sent for the doctor, who hurried to the palace with a joyful heart, not knowing what lay in store for him.

'Do you know why I have sent for you?' the King asked.

'God alone knows the unspoken thoughts of men,' the physician answered.

'I have brought you here to kill you,' said the King.

The physician was thunderstruck at these words.

'But why should you wish to kill me?' he cried. 'What is my crime?'

'It has come to my knowledge,' replied the King, 'that you have been sent here to cause my death. But you shall die first.'

Then he called in the executioner, saying, 'Strike off the head of this traitor!'

'Spare me, and Allah will spare you!' pleaded the unfortunate doctor. 'Kill me, and so will Allah kill you!'

But the King turned a deaf ear to his entreaties.

'Never will I have peace again,' he said, 'until I see you dead. For if you cured me by a thing held in the hand, you will doubtless kill me by the scent of a perfume, or by some other foul device.'

'Is it thus that you repay me?' the doctor protested. 'Will you thus repay good with evil?'

But the King said, 'You must now die; nothing now can save you.'

When he saw that the King had made up his mind to have him put to death, the physician bitterly repented the service he had done him. The executioner came forward, bandaged the doctor's eyes, and, drawing his sword, held it in readiness for the King's signal. But the doctor continued to plead. 'Spare me, and Allah will spare you! Kill me, and so will Allah kill you!'

Moved by the man's lamentations, one of the courtiers interceded for him.

'Spare the life of this man, I pray you,' he said to the King. 'He has committed no crime against you; rather has he cured you of an illness that your physicians had failed to remedy.'

'If I spare this doctor,' the King replied, 'he will use his devilish art to kill me. Therefore he must die.'

Once more the doctor repeated, 'Spare me, and Allah will spare you! Kill me, and so will Allah kill you!'

Realizing that the King was firmly fixed in his resolve, he said, 'Your Majesty, if you must kill me, I beg you to grant me a day's delay, so that I may go home and wind up my affairs. I want to say good-by to my family and my neighbors, and instruct them how to arrange my burial. I must also give away my books of medicine, among which there is one precious volume that I would offer to you as a parting gift, that you may preserve it among the treasures of your kingdom.'

'What may this book be?' the King asked.

'It holds secrets and devices without number, the least of them being this: that if, after you have struck off my head, you turn over three leaves of this book and read the first three lines upon the left-hand page, my severed head will speak and answer any questions you may ask it.'

The King was astonished to hear this, and at once ordered his guards to escort the physician home. That day the doctor put his affairs in order, and the next morning returned to the King's palace. There he found, already assembled, the ministers, the chamberlains, and all the chief officers of the realm. With their colored robes the court seemed like a garden full of flowers.

The doctor bowed low before the King; in one hand he held an ancient book, and in the other a little bowl filled with a strange powder. Then he sat down and said, 'Bring me a platter!'

A platter was instantly brought in, and the doctor sprinkled the powder on it and smoothed it over with his fingers. Then he handed the book to the King.

'Take this book,' he said, 'and set it down before you. When my head has been cut off, place it upon the powder to stop the bleeding. Then open the book.'

At the King's order, the executioner cut off the

physician's head with a single blow of his sword. Then the King opened the book and, finding the pages stuck together, put his finger to his mouth and turned over the first leaf. After much difficulty he turned over the second and the third, moistening his finger with his tongue each time, and tried to read. But there was no writing there.

'There is nothing written in this book,' cried the King.

'Go on turning,' replied the severed head.

The King had not turned six pages when the venom – for the leaves of the book were poisoned – began to work in his body. He fell backward in an agony of pain, crying, 'Poisoned! Poisoned!' and in a few moments he was dead.

'Now, faithless jinnee,' the fisherman went on, 'had the King spared the physician, he in turn would have been spared by Allah. But he refused, and Allah brought about the King's destruction. And as for you, if you had been willing to spare me, Allah would have been merciful to you, and I would have spared your life. But you sought to kill me; therefore I will throw you back into the sea and leave you to perish in this bottle!'

'Let me out! Let me out!' the jinnee cried. 'Do not be angry with me, I pray you. If I have done you evil, repay me with good and, as the saying goes, punish me with kindness. Do not do as the farmer did to the baker.'

'What is their story?' the fisherman asked.

'This bottle is no place to tell stories in,' exclaimed the jinnee, writhing with impatience. 'Let me out, and I will tell you all that passed between them.'

'Never!' the fisherman replied. 'I will throw you into the sea, and you shall remain imprisoned in your bottle till the end of time!'

'Let me out! Let me out!' moaned the jinnee in despair. 'I swear I will never harm you, and promise to render you a service that will enrich you!'

At last the fisherman accepted the jinnee's promise, made him swear by the Most High Name, and then opened the bottle with trembling hands.

At once the smoke burst out, and in a twinkling took the shape of a colossal jinnee, who with a triumphant kick sent the bottle flying into the sea. When the fisherman saw the bottle disappear, he was overcome with terror.

'This is a bad sign,' he thought; but, quickly hiding his anxiety, he said, 'Mighty jinnee, you have both promised and sworn that you would deal honorably with me. If you break your word, Allah will punish you. Remember that I said to you, as the physician said to the King, "Spare me, and Allah will spare you!"'

At this the jinnee laughed loud and long.

'Follow me!' he bellowed.

Still dreading the jinnee's intent, the fisherman followed him out of the city gates. They climbed a mountain and at length descended into a vast, barren valley in the middle of which there was a lake. At the shore of this lake the jinnee stopped in his tracks and bade the fisherman cast his net. The fisherman saw white fish and red fish, blue fish and yellow fish sporting in the water. Marveling at the sight, he cast his net into the lake, and when he drew it in, rejoiced to find in it four fish, each of a different color.

'Take these fish to the King's palace,' said the jinnee, 'and he will give you gold. In the meantime, I must beg you to pardon my ill manners, for I have dwelt so long at the bottom of the sea that I have forgotten the refinements of men. Come and fish in this lake each day – but only once a day. And now, farewell!'

So saying, the jinnee stamped his feet on the earth, which instantly opened and swallowed him up.

The fisherman went home, marveling at all that had happened to him. He filled an earthen bowl with water, placed the fish in it, and carried it on his head to the King's palace, as the jinnee had instructed.

When he had gained admission to the King's presence, the fisherman offered him the fish. The King, who had never seen their like in size or color, marveled greatly and ordered his vizier to take them to the cookmaid. The vizier took the fish to the slave girl and asked her to fry them. Then the King ordered his minister to give the fisherman four hundred pieces of gold. The fisherman received the coins in the lap of his robe, scarcely believing his good fortune. He bought bread and meat, and hurried home to his wife and children.

Meanwhile, the slave girl cleaned the fish, put them in the frying pan, and left them over the fire. When they were well cooked on one side, she turned them over; but scarcely had she done so when the wall of the kitchen suddenly opened and through it entered a beautiful young girl. She had dark eyes with long lashes, and smooth, fresh cheeks. She wore jeweled rings on her fingers and gold bracelets around her wrists, and her hair was wrapped in a blue-fringed kerchief of the rarest silk. The girl came forward and thrust into the frying pan a wand that she carried in her hand.

'Fish, fish, are you still faithful?' she asked.

At the sight of this apparition the slave fainted, and the young girl repeated her question a second and a third time. Then the four fishes lifted their heads from the pan and replied in unison, 'Yes, yes, we are faithful!'

Upon this the strange visitor overturned the pan and went out the way she had come, the wall of the kitchen closing behind her. When the slave girl came to her senses, she found the fish burned to cinders. She set up a great screaming and hurried to tell the vizier all that had happened. Amazed at her story, he sent immediately for the fisherman and ordered him to bring four other fish of the same kind. So the fisherman went off to the lake, cast his net, and caught four more fish. These he took to the vizier, who carried them to the slave girl, saying, 'Get up now and fry these in my presence.'

The slave cleaned the fish and put them in the frying pan; but scarcely had she done so when the wall opened as before and the girl reappeared, dressed in the same way and still holding the wand in her hand. She thrust the end of the wand into the pan and said, 'Fish, fish, are you still faithful?'

The four fish raised their heads and replied, 'Yes, yes, we are faithful!' And the girl overturned the pan with her wand and vanished through the wall.

'The king must be informed of this!' cried the vizier. He hurried to his master and recounted all that he had seen.

'I must see this myself,' said the astonished King.

He sent for the fisherman and ordered him to bring four more fish. The fisherman again hastened to the lake and promptly returned with the fish, for which he received four hundred pieces of gold. Then the King commanded his vizier to cook the fish in his presence.

'I hear and obey,' the vizier replied.

He cleaned the fish and set the pan over the fire; but scarcely had he thrown them in when the wall opened and there appeared a great giant. He held a green twig in his hand and, as soon as he set eyes on the pan, roared out, 'Fish, fish, are you still faithful?'

The four fish lifted their heads and replied, 'Yes, yes, we are faithful!'

Then the giant overturned the pan with his twig and disappeared through the chasm in the wall, leaving the four fish burned to black cinders.

Confounded at the sight, the King cried, 'I must find the answer to this riddle. No doubt these fish have some strange history.'

He sent again for the fisherman and asked him where he obtained the fish.

'From a lake between four hills,' replied the fisherman, 'beyond the mountain that overlooks this city.'

'How many days' journey is it?' asked the King.

'It is barely half an hour's walk, Your Majesty,' he answered.

The King set out for the lake at the head of his troops, accompanied by the bewildered fisherman, who led the way, muttering curses on the jinnee as he went. At last they came to the mountain and, after climbing to the top, descended into a great desert. They all marveled at the mountains, the lake, and the fish of different colors that swam in it. The King asked the troops if any of them had ever before seen a lake in that place, but they all replied that they had not.

'I swear I will never again enter my city or sit upon my throne,' he said, 'until I have solved the mystery of this lake and these colored fish.'

He ordered his troops to pitch tents for the

night and summoned his vizier, who was a wise counselor and a man of deep learning.

'Know,' he said to him, 'I have decided to go out alone tonight and search for the answer to the mystery of the lake and the fishes. I order you to stand guard at the door of my tent and tell anyone who may wish to see me that I am ill and cannot receive him. Above all, you must keep my plan secret.'

At nightfall the King disguised himself, girt on his sword, and slipped out of the camp unnoticed by his guards. All that night and throughout the following day he journeyed on, stopping only to rest awhile in the midday heat. Early the next morning he sighted a black building in the distance. He rejoiced and thought, 'There perhaps I will find someone who can explain the mystery of the lake and the fishes.'

When he drew near, he found that this was a towering palace built of black stone with iron. He went up to the great double door, one half of which was wide open, and knocked gently once, twice, and again, but heard no answer. The fourth time he knocked hard, but still received no reply. Supposing the palace to be deserted, he summoned up his courage and entered, calling out at the top of his voice, 'People of this house, have you any food for a weary traveler?' This he repeated again and again, and, getting no answer, passed to the center of the building. The hall was richly carpeted and hung with fine curtains and splendid tapestries. In the middle of the inner court a beautiful fountain, resting on four lions of red gold, spurted forth a jeweled spray, and about the fountain fluttered doves and pigeons under a golden net stretched above the courtyard.

The King marveled greatly at the splendor of all he saw, but grieved to find no one in the palace who could explain the mystery to him. As he was loitering thoughtfully about the court, however, he suddenly heard a low, mournful voice that seemed to come from a sorrowful heart. The King walked in the direction of the sound and presently came to a doorway concealed behind a curtain. Lifting the curtain, he saw a handsome young man, dressed in a gold-embroidered robe, lying on a bed in a spacious marble hall. His forehead was as white as a lily, and there was a black mole on his cheek.

The King was very glad to see the young man, and greeted him, saying, 'Peace be with you!' But the young man, whose eyes were sore with weeping, remained motionless on the bed and returned the King's greeting in a faint voice.

'Pardon me, sir, for not rising,' he murmured.

'Tell me the story of the lake and the fishes,' said the King, 'and the reason for your tears and your solitude.'

At these words the young man wept even more bitterly.

'How can I refrain from weeping,' he replied, 'condemned as I am to this unnatural state?'

So saying, he stretched out his hand and uncovered himself. The King was astonished to see that the lower half of his body was all of stone, while the upper half, from his waist to the hair upon his head, remained that of a living man.

'The story of the fishes,' said the youth, 'is indeed a strange tale. It is also my story, and the story of the fate that overtook this city and its people. I will tell it to you.'

The Tale of the Enchanted King

Know that my father was the King of a beautiful city that once flourished around this palace. His name was Mahmoud, and he was Lord of the Black Islands, which are now four mountains. He reigned for seventy years, and on his death I succeeded to the throne of his kingdom. I married my cousin, the daughter of my uncle, who loved me so passionately that she could not bear to part with me even for a moment. I lived happily with her for five years. It chanced one day, however, that my wife left the palace to visit the baths and was absent so long that I grew anxious for her safety. But I tried to dismiss my fears, and lay down on my couch, ordering two of my slave girls to fan me as I slept. One sat at my head and the other at my feet; and as I lay with my eyes closed I heard one say to the other, 'How unfortunate is the young King our master, and what a pity it is that he should have married our mistress, that hateful creature!'

'Allah's curse upon all enchantresses!' replied the other. 'This witch who spends her secret hours in the company of thieves and highwaymen is a thousandfold too vile to be the wife of our master.'

'And yet he must be blind not to see it,' said the first slave.

'But how should he suspect her,' returned the other, 'when every night she mixes in his cup a powerful drug that so affects his senses that he sleeps like the dead until morning? How can he know what she does and where she goes? After he has gone to sleep, she dresses and goes out of the palace, returning only at daybreak, when she wakes her husband with the aroma of an incense.'

When I heard this, my blood ran cold and I was dazed with horror. At dusk my wife came back to the palace, and we sat for an hour eating and drinking together as our custom was. At length I asked for the final cup that I drank every night before retiring. When she handed it to me, I lifted the cup to my lips but, instead of drinking, poured it quickly into the folds of my garments. Then I lay down on my bed and pretended to fall asleep.

Presently I heard her say, 'Sleep, and may you never wake again! Oh, how I despise you!'

She then dressed, tied my sword around her waist, and left the palace. I got up, put on a hooded cloak, and followed her. She stole away through the winding streets of the town and, on reaching the city gates, muttered a magic charm. Suddenly the heavy locks fell to the ground and the gates swung wide open. Without a sound I followed her out of the city until she came to a desolate wasteland and entered a ruined hovel topped by a dome. I climbed up to the roof and crouched over a chink in the ceiling. I saw her draw near an evil-looking ruffian who, judging by his appearance, could only have been a fugitive slave. When I saw them exchange greetings I was unable to control my rage. I jumped down from the roof, snatched the sword from my wife's belt, and struck the villain through the neck. A loud gasp shook his body. Thinking that the blow had killed him, I rushed out of the house and ran straight to the palace, where I tucked myself in bed and lay quite still. By and by, my wife returned and lay down quietly beside me.

Next morning I saw that my wife had cut off her tresses and dressed herself in deep mourning.

'Husband,' she said, 'do not be angry with me for wearing these clothes. I have just heard that my mother has died, that my father has lost his life in the holy war, that one of my brothers has been bitten to death by a serpent, and the other killed by the fall of a house. It is but right that I should weep and mourn.'

Showing no sign of anger, I replied, 'Do as you think fit. I shall not prevent you.'

She went in mourning for a whole week, and at the end of this time she had a dome built in the grounds of the palace. She called it the House of Grief, and to this monument she had her lover carried; for he was still alive, though dumb, and crippled in every limb. Every day, early and late, my wife took to him wine and stews and broths, and fell to wailing under the dome.

One day I entered her room and found her weeping and beating her face. Out of my mind with rage, I drew my sword and was about to strike her when she sprang to her feet and seemed suddenly to realize that it was I who had wounded her accomplice; she muttered a mysterious charm. 'Now, Powers of Magic,' she exclaimed, 'let half his body be turned to stone!'

At that moment I became as you see me now, neither alive nor dead. Then she bewitched my entire kingdom, turning its four islands into mountains with a lake in their midst and transforming all my subjects – Moslems, Jews, Christians, and heathens – into fishes of four different colors. Nor was she satisfied with this, for every day she comes to torture me; she gives me a hundred lashes with a leather thong and puts a shirt of haircloth on my wounds, all over the living part of my body.

⋆

When he had heard the young man's story, the King said to him, 'My son, your tale has added a heavy sorrow to my sorrows. But where is this enchantress now?'

'With her lover in the monument, which you can see from the door of this hall.'

'By Allah,' cried the King, 'I will do you a service that will be long remembered, a deed that will be recorded for all time.'

At midnight the King got up and, as the secret hour of sorcery was striking, stole away toward the monument with his sword unsheathed. Inside, he saw lighted lamps and candles, and braziers in which incense was burning. Before him lay the slave. Without a sound he stepped forward and struck him a mighty blow with his sword. The man fell dead upon the instant; and the King stripped him of his clothes, carried him on his shoulder, and threw him down a deep well in the grounds of the palace. Then he returned to the monument, put on the wretched man's clothes, and sat down with the sword hidden in the folds of his robe.

Shortly afterward the woman came into the monument carrying a cup of wine and a bowl of hot soup. As soon as she entered, she said, weeping, 'Speak to me, my master; let me hear your voice!'

Rolling his tongue in his mouth, the King replied in a low voice, 'There is no power or majesty except in Allah!'

When she heard the voice of her supposed friend, who had for so long been silent, the young witch uttered a joyful cry.

'Praise to the Highest!' she exclaimed. 'My master is restored!'

'Woman,' said the King in the same low voice, 'you are not worthy that I should speak to you!'

'Why, what have I done?' she asked.

'You have deprived me of all sleep,' he answered. 'Day after day you whip that husband of yours, so that his cries keep me awake all night. If you had had more thought for my comfort, I would have recovered long ago.'

'If it be your wish,' she replied, 'I will instantly restore him.'

'Do so,' said the King, 'and give me some peace.'

'I hear and obey,' answered the witch, and leaving the monument, hastened to the hall where the young man was lying. There she took a bowl filled with water, and, bending over it, murmured some magic words. The water began to seethe and bubble as if in a heated caldron; then she sprinkled it upon her husband and said, 'Now, Powers of Magic, return him to his natural state!'

A quiver passed through the young man's body and he sprang to his feet, shouting for joy, and crying, 'There is no god but Allah, and Mohammed is his Prophet!'

'Go,' shrieked his wife, 'and never return, or I will kill you!'

The young man hurried from her presence, and she came back to the monument.

'Rise up, my master,' she said, 'that I may look upon you!'

In a feeble voice the King replied, 'You have removed one part of the evil. The root cause still remains.'

'What may that be, my master?' she asked.

'The people of this enchanted city and the Four Islands,' he replied. 'Night after night, the fish raise their heads from the lake and call down curses upon us both. I will not be cured until they are delivered. Free them, and return to help me from my bed, for by that act I will be saved!'

Still taking him for her friend, she answered joyfully, 'I hear and obey!'

She hurried to the lake, and took a few drops of water in her palm; then she muttered some secret words. The spell was broken. The fish wriggled in the water and, raising their heads, changed back into human shape. The lake was turned into a bustling city, with people buying and selling in the market place; and the mountains became four islands.

Then the witch ran back to the palace and said to the King, 'Give me your hand, my master. Let me help you to your feet.'

'Come closer,' he murmured.

She drew near, and the King lifted his sword and thrust it into her breast, so that she fell down lifeless.

The King found the young man waiting for him at the palace gates. He congratulated him on his escape, and the youth kissed his hand and thanked him with all his heart. Then the King asked, 'Do you wish to stay in your own city or will you return with me to my kingdom?'

'Sir,' replied the youth, 'do you know how far your kingdom is from here?'

'Why, it is two and a half days' journey,' the King answered.

The young man laughed and said, 'If you are dreaming, Your Majesty, then you must wake. Know that you are at least a year's journey from your capital. If you came here in two days and a half, that was because my kingdom was enchanted ... But I will never leave you again, even for a moment.'

The King cried, 'Praise be to Allah, who has brought us together in this way. From now on, you shall be my son, for I have no child of my own.'

The two Kings embraced one another and rejoiced.

Returning to his palace, the younger King told his courtiers he intended to set out on a long journey. When all preparations were completed, the King set forth from the Black Islands, together with fifty slaves and fifty mules laden with priceless treasure. They journeyed for a whole year, and when at last they reached the capital, the vizier and the troops, who had abandoned all hope of the King's return, went out to meet their master and gave him a joyful welcome.

Seated upon the throne in his own palace, he summoned the vizier and his other courtiers, and told them about his adventure from beginning to end. Then he bestowed gifts on all who were present and said to the vizier, 'Send for the fisherman who brought us the colored fishes.'

The fisherman, who had been the means of freeing the enchanted city, was brought into his presence, and the King vested him with a robe of honor and asked him about his manner of life and whether he had any children. The fisherman replied that he had one son and two daughters. The King took one of the daughters in marriage and the young Prince wedded the other, while the fisherman's son was appointed royal treasurer. The vizier became Sultan of the Black Islands, and departed thither with fifty slaves and robes of honor for all the courtiers of that kingdom.

And so the King and the young Prince lived happily ever after. The fisherman became the richest man of his day, and his daughters were the wives of Kings until the end of their lives.

ALADDIN AND THE ENCHANTED LAMP

Once upon a time, there lived in a certain city of China a poor tailor who had an only son called Aladdin.

From his earliest years, Aladdin was a disobedient, lazy boy. When he was ten, his father wanted him to learn a trade; but as he was too poor to have the boy taught any other business than his own, he took him into his shop to teach him tailoring. Aladdin used to pass his time playing in the streets with other idle boys, and never stayed in the shop a single day. Whenever his father went out, or was attending to a customer, he would run off to the parks and gardens with little ruffians of his own age. He thus persisted in his senseless ways until his father fell ill with grief and died.

Seeing that her husband was dead and her son good for nothing, Aladdin's mother sold the shop with all its contents and took to cotton-spinning in order to support herself and her child. But the young rascal, no longer restrained even by the fear of a father, grew wilder than ever before. The whole day, except for meals, he spent away from home. And thus he carried on until he was fifteen years old.

One day, as he was playing in the street with his companions, a foreign-looking old man who was passing by stopped and watched Aladdin attentively. This stranger, who had come from the remotest parts of Morocco, in Africa, was a mighty enchanter, skilled in the science of the stars. He could, by the power of his magic, uproot a high mountain and hurl it down upon another. Having looked closely into Aladdin's face, he muttered to himself, 'This is the boy I have been seeking.'

He took one of the boys aside and asked him Aladdin's name, who Aladdin's father was, and where Aladdin lived. Then he went up to Aladdin and led him away from his friends.

'My child,' he said, 'are you not the son of Hassan the tailor?'

'Yes, sir,' Aladdin replied, 'but my father has been dead a long time.'

At these words the magician threw his arms around the boy's neck and kissed him again and again, with tears running down his cheeks.

'Why do you weep, sir?' asked Aladdin in bewilderment. 'Did you know my father?'

'How can you ask such a question, my child?' the magician replied in a sad, broken voice. 'How can I help weeping when I suddenly hear of my own brother's death? I have been traveling the world these many years, and now that I have returned in the hope of seeing him, you tell me, alas, that he is dead. But when I first saw you, your blood cried out that you were my brother's son. I recognized you at once, although when I left this land your father was not yet married. But alas, no man can escape his fate. My son,' he added, taking Aladdin again into his arms, 'you are now my only comfort; you stand in your father's place. Does not the proverb truly say: "He that leaves an heir does not die"?'

With that the magician took ten pieces of gold from his purse, gave them to Aladdin, and asked him where his mother lived. When the boy had directed him to the house, the magician said, 'Give this money to your mother, my dear brother's wife, with my kindest greetings. Tell her your uncle has returned from abroad and will visit her tomorrow. Say that I long to greet her, to see the house where my brother lived, and to look upon his grave.'

Aladdin was very glad to receive the money. He

kissed the magician's hand and ran home to his mother, arriving there long before suppertime.

'Good news, Mother!' he cried, bursting into the house. 'My uncle has come back from his travels and sends you his greetings.'

'Are you making fun of me, my child?' she answered. 'Who may this uncle be? And since when have you had a living relative?'

'How can you say I have no uncle or relations?' Aladdin protested. 'The man is my father's brother. He embraced me and kissed me, and wept bitterly when he heard that my father was dead. He has sent me to tell you of his arrival and of his wish to come and see you.'

'It is true, my son, that your father had a brother. But he is dead, and I never heard your father speak of any other.'

Next morning the magician left his lodgings and wandered about the town in search of Aladdin. He found him playing in the streets with his companions. Hurrying up to him, he embraced and kissed him as before and gave him two pieces of gold.

'Run along to your mother,' he said, 'and give her this money. Bid her prepare something for supper, and say that your uncle is coming to eat with you this evening. And now, my boy, show me the way to your house again.'

'Gladly, sir,' Aladdin replied; and after pointing out the road, he took the gold to his mother.

'My uncle is coming to have dinner with us this evening,' he told her.

Quickly she went to the market and bought all the food she needed. Then she borrowed pots and dishes from her neighbors and began to cook the meal. When evening came, she said to Aladdin, 'Dinner is ready, my son. Perhaps your uncle does not know his way about the town. Go out and see if you can find him in the street.'

Although Aladdin had pointed out to the magician the exact whereabouts of his mother's house, he was nevertheless very willing to go; but at that moment there came a knocking on the door. He ran to open it and found the magician standing on the doorstep and, with him, a porter laden with fruit and drink. Aladdin led him into the house, and after the porter was dismissed the magician greeted the boy's mother and begged her, with tears in his eyes, to show him where her husband used to sit. She showed him the place. He knelt down before it and kissed the ground.

'Alas, my poor brother!' he lamented. 'Oh, my sorrowful loss!'

His weeping convinced the woman that he really was her husband's brother. She helped him gently from the ground and spoke comforting words to him. And when all three were seated the magician began:

'Good sister, do not be surprised at not having seen or known me when my late brother was alive. It is now forty years since I left this land and began my wanderings in the far-flung regions of the earth. I traveled in India, Sind, and Arabia;

then I went to Egypt and stayed for a short time in the city of Cairo, the wonder of the world. Finally I journeyed into the deep interior of Morocco, and there I dwelt for thirty years. One day, as I was sitting all alone, I began to think of my native land and my only brother, and I was seized with a great longing to see him. I resolved to travel back to the country of my birth. I said to myself, "Perhaps your brother is poor, whereas, thank God, you are a man of wealth. Go, visit him, and help him in his need."

'I got up at once and made preparations for the journey. After saying my prayers, I mounted my horse and set forth. I experienced many hardships and perils before the Almighty brought me to this city. When I saw Aladdin my heart leaped for joy, for I recognized my nephew. But when he told me of my poor brother's death I nearly fainted from grief.'

Noticing that the poor woman was much affected by his words, the magician now changed the subject and, pursuing his plans, turned to the boy.

'Aladdin, my son, what trade have you learned? What business do you follow to support yourself and your mother?'

Aladdin hung his head.

'Oh, do not ask about Aladdin's trade!' his mother replied. 'By Allah, he knows nothing at all, nor have I ever seen a more worthless child. He wastes all his days with the young vagabonds of the streets. It was he who sent his poor father to his grave, and I myself shall follow him soon. Day and night I toil at the spinning wheel to earn a couple of loaves for us. Why, he never comes home except for meals! That is all I see of him. I have a good mind to turn him out of doors and leave him to fend for himself; for I am getting old and have not the strength to wear myself out as I used to do.'

'That is not right, my boy,' the magician said; 'such conduct is unworthy of a fine young man like yourself. It does you little credit to let your mother work to keep you, when you are old enough to support yourself. Learn a trade so that you will have the skill to earn a living. Perhaps you did not like your father's trade; choose another that you fancy, and I will do all I can to help you.'

Aladdin remained silent, and the magician, realizing that he still preferred his idle life, went on, 'Very well, my boy. If you have no mind to learn a trade, there is no harm in that. I will open a shop for you in the town and furnish it with silks and linens, so that you soon become a respected merchant.'

Aladdin was pleased with the prospect of being a merchant dressed in splendid clothes. He smiled at the magician and nodded his head in approval of this plan.

'Now, nephew,' the magician went on, 'tomorrow I will take you, God willing, to the market and buy you a fine merchant's suit. Then we will look for a suitable shop.'

Deeply impressed by all the good things the magician promised to do for her son, Aladdin's mother thanked him heartily. She begged the boy to mend his ways and show obedience to his uncle. Then she got up and served the meal. As the three ate and drank, the magician chatted with Aladdin about trade and business affairs. When the night was far advanced, the magician departed, promising to return next morning.

Aladdin could scarcely sleep for joy. In the morning there was a knocking on the door and Aladdin ran out to meet the magician. He greeted him and kissed his hand, and they went off together to the market place. Entering a shop, stocked with clothes of every description, the magician asked to be shown the most expensive suits and told Aladdin to choose the one he fancied. The boy picked out a magnificent outfit, for which the magician paid without haggling. From there they went to the city baths, and after they had washed and refreshed themselves, Aladdin put on his new clothes and rejoiced to see himself so finely dressed. Beaming with delight, he kissed his uncle's hand and thanked him with all his heart.

Then the magician led Aladdin to the merchant's bazaar, where he saw the traders buying and selling in their stores.

'My son,' he said, 'as you are soon to be a merchant like these men, it is but proper that you should frequent this market and get acquainted with the people.'

He showed him the sights of the city, the great buildings and the mosques, and at midday took him to an inn, where they were served a meal on plates of silver. They ate and drank until they were satisfied; and then the magician took Aladdin to see the Sultan's palace and the surrounding parks. After that he took him to the foreign merchants' inn where he himself was staying, and invited a number of his friends to dinner. When they came he introduced Aladdin to them as his brother's son.

At nightfall he took him back to his mother. The poor woman was transported with joy when she saw her son dressed like a merchant, and called down a thousand blessings on the magician.

'Brother,' she said, 'I do not know how to thank you for your kindness. May Allah prolong your life for both our sakes.'

'Dear sister-in-law,' the magician replied, 'I have done nothing to deserve your thanks. Aladdin is my son; I am in duty bound to be a father to him. He is no longer a child but a man of sense. It is my dearest wish that he should do well and be a joy to you in your old age. I am very sorry, however, that, tomorrow being Friday, the market will be closed and I will not be able to open a shop for him as I promised. But, God willing, we shall do that the day after. I will come here tomorrow to take Aladdin with me and show him the parks and gardens beyond the city.'

The magician then said good-by and went back to his lodgings.

Aladdin thought of his good fortune and the delights that were in store for him. For he had never been out of the city gates before, or seen the countryside beyond. Next morning he got up early, and as soon as he heard a knocking on the door, he ran to receive his uncle. The magician took him into his arms and kissed him.

'Today, dear nephew,' he said, 'I will show you some fine things, the like of which you have never seen in all your life.'

Hand in hand they walked along until they came out of the city gates and reached the fine parks and tall palaces that lay beyond. Aladdin exclaimed for joy as they came in sight of each different building. When they had walked a long way from the city and were tired out, they entered a beautiful garden and sat down to rest beside a fountain of crystal water, surrounded by bronze lions as bright as gold. Here the magician untied a bundle that hung from his belt and took out of it various fruits and pastries.

'Eat, nephew, for you must be hungry,' he said.

After they had eaten and rested they walked on through the gardens until they reached the open country and came to a high mountain.

'Where are we going, uncle?' asked Aladdin, who had never walked so far in all his days. 'We have now passed all the gardens, and there is nothing before us except that mountain. Please let us go home, for I am worn out with walking.'

'Be a man, my boy,' the magician replied. 'I

want to show another garden more beautiful than any you have yet seen. No king has the like of it in the whole world.'

And to engage Aladdin's attention, he told him strange stories, until they reached the goal that the magician had set himself. To see that spot he had come all the way from Morocco to China.

'Here I am going to show you strange and wondrous things such as the eyes of man have never seen before,' he said to Aladdin.

He allowed the boy to rest awhile and then said to him, 'Rise now and gather up some dry sticks and fragments of wood so that we may light a fire. Then you shall see the marvel that I have brought you here to witness.'

Wondering what his uncle was about to do, Aladdin forgot how tired he was and went into the bushes in search of dry twigs. He gathered up a great armful and carried them to the old man. Presently the magician set fire to the wood and, when it was ablaze, opened a small box he had with him and threw a pinch of incense from it into the flame, muttering a secret charm. At once the sky was overcast with darkness and the earth shook and opened before him, revealing a marble slab with a copper ring fixed in the center. The boy was terrified at these happenings and wanted to run away; but the magician, who could never hope to achieve his aim without Aladdin's help, caught hold of him and, raising his fist, gave him a mighty blow on the head that almost knocked out some of his teeth. Aladdin fell back fainting; nor did he recover his senses until the magician revived him by magic.

'What have I done to deserve this, uncle?' Aladdin sobbed, trembling in every limb.

'I struck you to make a man of you, my child,' replied the magician in a gentle tone. 'I am your uncle, your father's brother, and you must obey me. If you do as I tell you, you will be richer than all the monarchs of the world. Now listen carefully to my instructions. You have just seen how I opened the earth by my magic. Below this marble slab there is a treasure house that none but yourself may enter. Only you can lift the stone and go down the stairs that lie beneath. Do as I tell you, and we will divide the hidden riches between us.'

Aladdin was amazed at the magician's words. He forgot his tears and the smarting blow he had received.

'Tell me what to do, uncle,' he cried, 'and I will obey you.'

The magician went up to him and kissed him. 'Nephew,' he said, 'you are dearer to me than a son. To see you a fine rich man is my utmost wish. Come, take hold of that ring and lift it.'

'But, uncle,' Aladdin replied, 'I am not strong enough to lift it alone. Come and help me.'

'No, my boy,' said the magician. 'If I help you we will gain nothing and all our labors will be lost. Try by yourself and you will find you can lift it with the greatest ease. Just take hold of the ring, and as you raise it pronounce your name, and your father's and mother's.'

Aladdin summoned up all his strength and did as the magician had told him. The slab moved easily under his hand; he set it aside, and down below he saw a vaulted cave with a stairway of a dozen steps leading to the entrance.

'Now be careful, Aladdin,' the magician cried. 'Do exactly as I tell you, and omit nothing. Go down into the cave, and at the bottom you will find a great hall divided into four rooms. In each room you will see four gold coffers and other precious things of gold and silver. Walk straight on and take care not to touch the coffers or the walls, even with the skirt of your gown; for if you do you will at once be changed into black stone. When you reach the fourth room you will find another door, which opens onto a beautiful garden shaded with fruit trees. Pronounce the names you spoke over the slab and make your way through it. After walking some fifty yards you will come to a staircase of about thirty steps, leading up to a terrace. On the terrace you will find a lamp. Take down the lamp, pour out the oil in it, and put it away in the breast of your robe. Do not worry about your clothes, for the oil is no ordinary oil. On your way back you may pause among the trees and pluck off whatever fruit you fancy.'

When he had finished speaking, the magician drew a ring from his finger and put it on one of Aladdin's.

'This ring, my boy,' he said, 'will deliver you from all dangers, so long as you do what I have told you. Be bold and resolute, and fear nothing. You are now a man, and not a child any more. In a few moments you will be the richest man alive.'

Aladdin jumped down into the cave and found the four rooms with the four gold coffers in each. Bearing in mind the magician's instructions, he cautiously made his way through them and came out into the garden. From there he climbed up the staircase to the terrace, took down the lamp, poured out the oil, and put the lamp into the breast of his robe. Then he returned to the garden and stopped for the first time to admire the trees and the singing birds that perched upon the branches. The trees were laden with fruit of every shape and hue: white, red, green, yellow, and other colors. Now, Aladdin was too young to realize that these were pearls and diamonds, emeralds and rubies, and jewels such as no king ever possessed. He took them for colored glass of little value, and yet was so delighted with their brilliance that he gathered a great quantity of them and stuffed them into his pockets and the folds of his belt and gown. When he had loaded himself with as much as he could carry, he hurried back through the four rooms without touching the gold coffers and quickly climbed the staircase at the cavern's mouth. But because of his heavy load he could not climb the last step, which was higher than the others.

'Uncle,' he shouted, 'give me your hand and help me up.'

'My dear boy,' the magician replied, 'you will do better first to give me the lamp. It is in your way.'

The magician, whose only concern was to get hold of the lamp, persisted in his demand. Aladdin, on the other hand, had so burdened himself that he could not get at it, and was therefore unable to give it to him. Provoked by the obstinate refusal of the boy, who, he thought, wanted the lamp for himself, the magician flew into a terrible rage. He ran to the blazing fire, threw more incense upon it, and howled a magic charm. At once the marble slab moved into its place and the earth closed over the cave, leaving Aladdin underground.

Now, as I told you before, the old man was really a stranger and no uncle of Aladdin's. He was an evil magician from the darkest part of Morocco, an African skilled in the renowned black arts of his native land. From his earliest days he had given himself up to sorcery and witchcraft, so that after forty years' continuous study he discovered that near one of the remotest cities of China there was a vast treasure, the like of which no king had ever amassed. He had also learned that the treasure included an enchanted lamp that could make him richer and more powerful than any monarch in the world, and that it could be brought out only by a boy of humble birth called Aladdin, a native of that city. Convinced of his discovery, he set out for China and, after a long and arduous journey, sought out Aladdin and reached the place where the treasure was buried. But all his efforts having failed, he imprisoned the boy underground, so that neither he nor the lamp should ever come up out of the earth. Then the magician abandoned his quest and journeyed back to Africa with a heavy heart. So much for him.

As for Aladdin, when the earth closed over him, he realized he had been deceived, and that the magician was no uncle of his. Giving up all hope of escape, he went down weeping to the bottom of the stairs and groped his way in the dark to the garden; but the door, which had been opened by enchantment, was now shut by the same means. He returned to the entrance of the cave in despair and threw himself on the steps. There he sat for three long days without food or drink, and almost abandoned all hope of living. He wept and sobbed, wrung his hands, and prayed for God's help with all his heart. While he was wringing his hands together he happened to rub the ring that the magician had given him as a protection.

At once a great black jinnee appeared before him.

'I am here, master, I am here,' the jinnee cried. 'Your slave is ready to serve you. Ask what you will and it shall be done. For I am the slave of him who wears my master's ring.'

The sight of this monstrous figure struck terror

into Aladdin's heart. But, as he recalled the magician's words, his hopes revived and he summoned up all his courage.

'Slave of the ring,' he cried, 'I order you to carry me up to the earth's surface.'

The words were scarcely out of his mouth when the earth was rent asunder and he found himself above ground on the very spot where the marble slab had been. It was some time before his eyes could bear the light after being so long in total darkness; but at length he looked about him and was amazed to see no sign of the cave or entrance. He would not have recognized the place but for the black cinders left by the magician's fire. In the distance he saw the city shimmering amid its gardens and hastened joyfully toward it, greatly relieved at his escape. He reached home worn out with hunger and fatigue, and dropped down fainting before his mother, who, for her part, had been grieving bitterly. The poor woman did all she could to restore her son; she sprinkled water over his face and gave him fragrant herbs to smell. As soon as he came to, he asked for something to eat.

'Mother, I am very hungry,' he said. 'I have had nothing to eat or drink these three days.'

His mother brought him all the food that she could find in the house, and when he had eaten and recovered his strength a little he said, 'You must know, Mother, that the man whom we supposed to be my uncle is a magician, a wicked imposter, a cruel fiend. He made me those promises only to destroy me. To think how we were deceived by his fine words! Listen, Mother, to what he did . . .'

And with that, Aladdin proceeded to tell his mother of his adventure with the magician from beginning to end.

When she had heard his story, Aladdin's mother shook her head.

'I might have known from the very start that the old wretch was a liar and a fraud. Praise be to God, who has delivered you from his hands.'

She went on comforting him in this way until Aladdin, who had not slept a wink for three days, was overcome by sleep. He did not wake till nearly noon the following day, and as soon as he opened his eyes he asked for food.

'Alas, my boy,' his mother sighed, 'I have not a crust of bread to give you; yesterday you ate all the food I had. But be patient a little. I have some cotton here that I have spun. I will go and sell it to buy you something to eat.'

'Leave your cotton for the time, Mother,' Aladdin answered, 'and give me the lamp I brought. I will sell it in the market, for it is sure to fetch a better price than your spinning.'

Aladdin's mother brought him the lamp and, noticing that it was dirty, said, 'If we clean and polish it, it might fetch a little more.'

She mixed a little sand in water and began to clean the lamp. But no sooner had she rubbed the surface than a tall and fearsome jinnee appeared before her.

'What is your wish, mistress?' said the jinnee. 'I am your slave and the slave of him who holds the lamp. I and the other slaves of the lamp will do your bidding.'

The poor woman, who was not used to such apparitions, was so terrified that she could not answer; her tongue became knotted in her mouth and she fell fainting to the ground. Now, Aladdin had seen the jinnee of the ring in the cave, and when he heard this jinnee speaking to his mother he ran quickly to her aid and snatched the lamp out of her hands.

'Slave of the lamp,' he said, 'I am hungry. Bring me some good things to eat.'

The jinnee vanished, and in a twinkling reappeared, carrying upon his head a priceless tray of solid silver that held twelve dishes of the choicest meats, together with a pair of silver goblets, two flasks of clear old wine, and bread as white as snow. All these he set down before Aladdin and disappeared again.

Seeing that his mother still lay unconscious on the floor, Aladdin sprinkled rose water over her face and gave her fragrant scents to smell.

'Get up, Mother,' he said, when she came to. 'Let us sit down and eat.'

Seeing the massive silver tray and the food upon it, she asked in amazement, 'Who may this generous benefactor be who has discovered our poverty and hunger? We are surely grateful to him for his kindness. Is it the Sultan himself who has heard of our wretched plight and sent us this tray?'

'Mother,' Aladdin replied, 'this is no time to ask questions. Get up and let us eat. We are starving.'

They sat at the tray and fell to heartily. Aladdin's mother had never in all her life tasted such delicate food, which was worthy of a king's table. Nor did they know whether the tray was valuable or not, for they had never seen such things before. They ate until they were satisfied; yet enough was left over for supper and the next day. Then they got up, washed their hands, and sat chatting.

'Now, my child,' said Aladdin's mother, 'tell me what you did with the jinnee.'

Aladdin told his mother what had passed between him and the jinnee from the time she fainted.

'I have heard,' said the astonished woman, 'that these creatures do appear to men, but I never saw any before this. He must be the same jinnee who rescued you in the cavern.'

'No, Mother,' Aladdin answered. 'That was a different jinnee. The jinnee that appeared to you was the jinnee of the lamp.'

'How is that, my child?' she asked.

'This jinnee was of a different shape,' replied Aladdin. 'The other was the slave of the ring; the one you saw belonged to the lamp that you were holding.'

'My child,' she cried, 'I beg you to throw away

both the lamp and the ring. I am terrified of those beings, and could not bear to see them again. Besides, it is unlawful for us to have any dealings with them.'

'I would gladly obey you in anything, Mother,' Aladdin replied, 'but I cannot afford to lose the lamp or the ring. You have yourself seen how useful the lamp was to us when we were hungry. And remember: when I went down into the cave, that imposter of a magician did not ask me for gold and silver, although the four rooms of the treasure house were full of them. He told me to fetch him the lamp and nothing else; for he must have known its great value. That is why we must keep this lamp and take good care of it, for in having it we will never again be poor or hungry. Also, we must never show it to anyone. As for the ring – I could not bear to lose that, either. But for its jinnee, I would have died under the earth, inside the treasure house. Who knows what troubles and dangers the future holds for me? This ring will surely save my life. Still, I will hide the lamp away if you like, so that you need never set eyes on it again.'

'Very well, my boy,' said his mother, finding his arguments reasonable enough. 'Do as you please. For my part, I will have nothing to do with them, nor do I wish ever to see that fearsome sight again.'

For two days they went on eating the food the jinnee had brought them; and when it was finished, Aladdin took one of the dishes from the magic tray and went to sell it in the market. There he was approached by a crafty old silversmith. Aladdin, who did not know that it was solid silver, offered him the plate; and when the silversmith saw it, he drew the boy aside so that no one else should see it. He examined the dish with care and found that it was made of the purest silver, but did not know whether Aladdin was aware of its true value.

'How much do you want for it, sir?' asked the silversmith.

'*You* should know how much it is worth,' Aladdin answered. Hearing the boy's businesslike reply, the silversmith was at a loss. He was at first tempted to offer him very little, but feared that Aladdin might know its value. Then he was inclined to give him a substantial sum. At last he took out one piece of gold from his pocket and offered it to him. When Aladdin saw the piece of gold he took it and ran off in great joy, so that the old man, realizing that the boy had no idea of its value, bitterly regretted that he had not given him less.

Aladdin hurried away to the baker's and bought some bread; then he ran home and gave the bread and the change to his mother. 'Mother,' he said, 'go and buy what we need.'

His mother went down to the market and bought all the food they needed; and the two ate until they had had enough. Whenever the money ran out, Aladdin would go to the market and sell another dish to the silversmith, and thus the old rogue bought all the plates for very little. Even then he would have wished to give him less; but having rashly paid him one piece of gold on the first occasion, he feared that the boy would go and sell elsewhere. When the twelve dishes were all gone, Aladdin decided to sell the silver tray. As this was large and heavy, he fetched the old merchant to the house and showed it to him. The silversmith, seeing its tremendous size, gave him ten pieces. And with this money Aladdin and his mother were able to provide for their needs several days longer.

When the gold was finished Aladdin took out the lamp and rubbed it, and the jinnee appeared before him. 'Master,' he said, 'ask what you will. I am your slave and the slave of him who holds the lamp.'

'I order you,' said Aladdin, 'to bring me a tray of food like the one you brought before. I am hungry.'

The jinnee vanished, and in the twinkling of an eye returned with a tray exactly like the first one, holding twelve splendid dishes full of delicate meats, two flasks of wine, and a fine, clean loaf. Having been warned beforehand, Aladdin's mother had left the house so that she would not see the jinnee; but when she returned and saw the tray with the silver dishes, and smelled the rich aroma, she marveled greatly and rejoiced.

'Look, Mother!' Aladdin cried. 'You told me to throw the lamp away. Now see how valuable it is.'

'You are right, my son,' she replied. 'Still, I do not want ever to see that jinnee again.'

She sat down with her son and the two ate and drank together. What was left over they stored for the following day. When this was finished, Aladdin took one of the dishes under his robe and went off to search for the silversmith. It chanced, however, that while he was walking through the market he passed by the shop of an honest goldsmith, well known for his integrity and fair dealing. The old sheikh stopped Aladdin and greeted him.

'What brings you here, my son?' he asked. 'I have often seen you pass this way and do business with a certain silversmith. I have watched you give him some articles, and perhaps you have something with you now that you intend to sell to him. You do not seem to realize, my child, that this man is a scoundrel and a cheat. What an easy prey he must have found you! If you have something to sell, show it to me and I will pay you the proper price for it: not a copper less.'

Aladdin showed him the plate, and the goldsmith took it and weighed it in his scales.

'Have you been selling him plates like this one?' asked the old man.

'Yes,' Aladdin replied.

'How much have you been getting for them?'

'One piece of gold for each,' Aladdin answered.

'What a rascal,' exclaimed the goldsmith, 'to rob honest folk in this way! You must know, my boy, that this man has swindled you and made a real fool of you. This dish is made of the purest silver and is worth no less than seventy pieces. If you are willing to accept this price, take it.'

The goldsmith counted out seventy pieces, and Aladdin took the gold and thanked the old man for his kindness. In due course he sold him the other dishes, at the same honest price. The youth and his mother grew very rich, yet they continued to live modestly, avoiding extravagance and foolish waste.

Aladdin had now given up his idle ways and bad companions and passed all his time in the markets of the city, speaking with persons of distinction and merchants great and small. He also visited the bazaars of the goldsmiths and jewelers, where he would sit and watch the jewels being bought and sold. As the months passed by, he came to realize that the varied fruits he had brought back from the treasure house were not colored glass or crystal but gems beyond the wealth of kings. He examined all the jewels in the market, but found none to be compared with the smallest of his own. Thus he went on visiting jewelers' shops, so that he might become acquainted with the people and learn from them the affairs of trade. He asked them questions about buying and selling, taking and giving, and in time came to know what was cheap and what was costly.

It so chanced that one morning, while he was on his way to the jewelers' market, he heard a herald crying in the streets, 'By command of our Royal Master, the Sultan! Let all people close their shops and retire at once behind the doors of their houses; for the Princess Badr-al-Budur, the Sultan's daughter, desires this day to visit the baths. If anyone disregards this order he shall be punished by instant death.'

When he heard this proclamation, Aladdin was seized with a great desire to see the Sultan's daughter, for her loveliness was the talk of all the people. He began casting around for some way to look upon her, and at last decided that it was best to stand behind the door of the baths and see her face as she entered. Without losing a moment, he ran straight off to the baths and hid himself behind the great door where none could see him. Presently the Princess left the palace and, after riding through the streets and seeing the sights of the city, halted at the baths. She lifted her veil as she went in. Her face shone like the radiant sun.

'Truly,' murmured Aladdin to himself, 'she is a credit to her Maker! Praise be to him who created her and gave her such beauty.' He fell in love with her immediately.

Many a time he had heard tell of Badr-al-Budur's beauty, but he had never imagined her to be so lovely. He returned home in a daze. His mother questioned him anxiously, but he said nothing; she brought him his dinner, but he refused to eat.

'What has come over you, my child?' she asked. 'Are you ill? Have you any pain? Tell me, my son, I beg you.'

'Let me alone, Mother,' he replied.

She went on pressing him to eat, and at last he ate a little. Then he threw himself upon his bed, where he lay thinking about the Princess all night and throughout the following day. His mother grew anxious about him and said, 'If you are in pain, my child, tell me and I will call the doctor. There is now an Arab doctor in our city; he was sent for by the Sultan. People everywhere are talking of his great skill. Shall I go and fetch him for you?'

'I am not ill,' Aladdin replied. 'It is only this, Mother. Yesterday I saw the Princess Badr-al-Budur when she was going into the baths. I saw her face, for when she entered she lifted her veil. As I looked on her exquisite features, my heart quivered with love for her. I will have no rest until I have won her in marriage from her father the Sultan.'

Hearing this, his mother thought he had gone mad.

'Heaven protect you, my child!' she exclaimed. 'You must be out of your mind. Come, return to your senses.'

'I am not mad, Mother,' Aladdin replied. 'Whatever you say, I will never change my mind. I cannot rest until I win the fair Badr-al-Budur, the treasure of my heart.'

'Do not say such things,' his mother implored. 'If the neighbors hear you they will think you are insane. Why, who would demand such a thing of the Sultan? And even if you do decide to ask for her hand, who will have the audacity to present your suit?'

'Who else should present my suit for me when I have you, Mother?' he answered. 'Whom can I trust more than you? I want you yourself to go and take my petition to the Sultan.'

'Heaven preserve me from such folly!' she exclaimed. 'Do you think I am mad, too? Consider who you are, my child. Your father was the poorest tailor in this city, and I, your mother, come from scarcely nobler folk. How then can you presume to demand the Sultan's daughter? Her father will marry her only to some illustrious prince no less powerful and noble than himself.'

'I have thought about all this, Mother,' replied Aladdin. 'Nothing will turn me from my purpose. If you love me as your son, I beg you to do this kindness for me. Do not let me perish; for I will surely die if I fail to win my heart's beloved. Remember, Mother. I am your son.'

'Yes, my son,' she said. 'You are my only child. My dearest wish is to see you married, and to rejoice in your happiness. If you want to marry, I will find you a wife who is your equal. But even then I will not know how to answer when they ask me if you have any trade or property. And if I cannot give an answer to humble people like ourselves, how can I presume to ask the Sultan for his only daughter? Just think of it, my child. Who is it that wants to marry her? A tailor's son! Why, I know for sure that if I speak of such a thing we shall be utterly ruined; it may even put us in danger of our lives. Besides, how can I gain access to the Sultan? If they ask me questions, what answer can I give them? And supposing that I do gain admittance to the Sultan, what gift can I present him with? Yes, my son, I know that our Sultan is very kind, but he bestows his favors only on those who deserve them. Now tell me, child, what have you done for the Sultan or his kingdom to be worthy of such a favor?'

'What you say is quite true, Mother,' Aladdin replied. 'You ask me what present I have to offer the Sultan. Know then that I can offer him a gift the like of which no monarch has ever possessed. Those colored fruits that I brought with me from the treasure house, thinking them to be glass or crystal, are jewels of incalculable worth – not a king in the world has the least one of them. I have been going around with jewelers of late, and I know now that they are priceless gems. If you wish to judge them for yourself, bring me a large china dish and I will show you. I am convinced that with a present such as this your errand will be easy.'

Half in doubt, the woman went and brought a large china dish. She set it before Aladdin, who took out the jewels from their hiding place and ranged them skillfully on the plate. As she looked upon them, her eyes were dazzled by their rich luster.

'Don't you see, Mother? Can there be a more magnificent present for the Sultan? I have no doubt that you will be well received and highly honored by him. Rise now, take the dish, and go to the Sultan's palace.'

'Yes, my son,' she answered. 'I admit that your present is both precious and unique. But who in heaven's name could make so bold as to stand before the Sultan and demand his daughter? When he asks, "What do you want?" my courage will fail me and I will not know what to say. And suppose the Sultan were pleased to accept your present and asked me, as people do on such occasions, about your standing and your income, what would I tell him?'

'The Sultan will never ask you such a question after seeing these splendid jewels,' Aladdin replied. 'Do not trouble your mind with groundless fears, but go boldly about your errand and offer him these gems. And remember: I have a lamp that brings me whatever I want. If the Sultan asks you such a question, the lamp will provide me with the answer.'

They went on chatting together for the rest of that evening. In the morning, Aladdin's mother made ready for her audience with a cheerful heart, now that she understood the properties of the lamp and all that it could do for them. After

Aladdin had made her promise never to reveal the secret, she wrapped the dish of gems in a handsome shawl and set off for the Sultan's palace at an early hour, so that she might enter the audience hall before it was crowded. When she arrived, the hall was not yet full. After a short while the ministers and courtiers, the nabobs and princes and great ones of the palace came in; then the Sultan himself entered, and everyone stood up in respectful silence. The great Sultan sat down on his throne, and at his bidding all present took their seats, according to their rank.

The petitioners were now summoned before the throne and every case was judged upon its merits; but the greater part of them had to be dismissed for lack of time. Among these last was Aladdin's mother, for, though she had arrived before the others, no one spoke to her or offered to take her before the Sultan. When the audience was finished and the Sultan had retired, she returned home. Aladdin, who was waiting on the doorstep, saw her come back with the present in her hand, but said nothing and waited until she came in and told him what had happened.

'Be of good cheer, my son,' she said at last. 'I plucked up enough courage to enter the audience hall today, though, like many others, I could not speak to the Sultan. But have no fears: God willing, I will speak to him tomorrow.'

Though vexed at the delay, Aladdin found comfort in his mother's words and consoled himself with hope and patience. Next morning the woman took the present and went again to the Sultan's palace, but found the audience chamber closed. The guards told her that the Sultan held an audience only three times a week, so she was obliged to return home. After that she went to the palace every day. When she found the hall open she would stand about helplessly and then, when the audience was finished, would make her way home; on the other days she would find the hall closed. This went on for a whole week. At the end of the final session the Sultan said to his vizier as they left the court, 'For six or seven days I have seen a poor woman come to the palace with something under her cloak. What does she want?'

'Some trivial matter, I expect, Your Majesty,' answered the vizier. 'She probably has a complaint against her husband or one of her neighbors.'

The Sultan, however, would not be put off by this reply. He ordered the vizier to bring the woman before him if she came once more.

'I hear and obey, Your Majesty,' answered the vizier, lifting his hand to his brow.

Next morning, the Sultan saw Aladdin's mother standing wearily in the audience hall, as on the previous days.

'That is the woman about whom I spoke to you yesterday,' he said to the vizier. 'Bring her to me now, so that I can hear her petition and grant her request.'

The vizier rose at once and led Aladdin's mother

before the Sultan. She fell on her knees and, kissing the ground before him, wished him long life and everlasting glory.

'Woman,' said the Sultan, 'I have seen you come to the audience hall a number of times and stand there without a word. Make your request known to me that I may grant it.'

Aladdin's mother again called down blessings upon the Sultan and, once more kissing the ground, said, 'Before I speak of the extraordinary cause that compels me to appear before you, I beg Your Majesty to pardon and forgive the boldness of the plea I am about to make.'

Being of a kind and generous nature, the Sultan ordered the audience chamber to be cleared so that she might be free to explain herself. When all but the vizier had been dismissed, he turned to Aladdin's mother and bade her speak out without fear.

'I have a son who is called Aladdin, Your Majesty,' she began. 'One day he heard the crier proclaim through the streets that Princess Badr-al-Budur was going to the baths. He was so anxious to see her face that he hid himself behind the door of the baths and saw her as she went in. He loved her from that instant, and has not known a moment's rest ever since. My son asked me to entreat Your Majesty to marry her to him; and, try as I might, I could not free his mind of this obsession. "Mother," he said to me, "if I do not win the Princess in marriage I will die." I beg you, great Sultan, to be indulgent and to forgive me and my son for the audacity of this request.'

When she had finished speaking the Sultan laughed good-naturedly.

'Now tell me what you are carrying in that bundle,' he said. Noticing that the Sultan was not angry, Aladdin's mother undid the shawl and presented him with the plate of jewels. At once the entire hall was lit up as if by chandeliers and colored torches. The dumbfounded Sultan gazed at the jewels and marveled at their brilliance, their size, and their beauty.

'Never in all my life have I seen the like of these jewels!' he exclaimed. 'I do not think there is a single stone in my treasuries to be compared with them. What do you say, vizier? Have you ever seen such marvels?'

'Never, Your Majesty,' agreed the vizier. 'I doubt if the smallest of them is to be found among your treasures.'

'Then do you not think,' said the Sultan, 'that the young man who sent them to me is worthier of my daughter's hand than any other?'

The vizier was greatly troubled to hear this, and did not know what to answer; for the Sultan had promised Badr-al-Budur to his own son.

'Great Sultan,' he said in a whisper, 'forgive me if I remind Your Majesty that you have promised the Princess to my son. I therefore beg you to allow him a delay of three months in which to find, with God's help, a present more valuable than this.'

The Sultan knew well enough that neither the vizier nor the richest king in the world could find him a present equal to the treasure he had just received; but, as he did not wish to offend his minister, he granted him the delay he had requested.

'Go to your son,' he said, turning to Aladdin's mother, 'and tell him that my daughter shall be his. Only the marriage cannot take place for three months, as there are preparations to be made.'

She thanked the Sultan and called down blessings upon him, then hurried home in a transport of joy. When Aladdin saw her return without the present, and noticed her happy smile, he felt sure she had brought him good news.

'I pray that the jewels have won the Sultan's heart,' he exclaimed. 'He received you graciously and listened to your request, I hope.'

His mother told him how the Sultan had accepted the jewels and marveled at their size and beauty.

'He promised that the Princess should be yours,' she went on. 'But the vizier whispered something to him and after that he said the marriage could not take place for three months. My son, I fear that the vizier may use his cunning to change the Sultan's mind.'

Ignoring this fear, Aladdin was overjoyed at the Sultan's promise and warmly thanked his mother for her labors.

'Surely now I am the richest and happiest of men!' he exclaimed.

For two months Aladdin patiently counted the days that separated him from the great occasion. Then, one evening, his mother went out to buy some oil and, as she walked down the street, she noticed that most of the shops were closed and that the city was adorned with lights. Windows were hung with flowers and candles, and the squares thronged with troops and mounted dignitaries carrying torches. Puzzled by all this, the old woman entered an oil shop that was open and, after buying what she needed, asked the reason for the commotion.

'Why, good woman!' replied the oil vendor. 'You must surely be a stranger here, not to know that this is the bridal night of Princess Badr-al-Budur and the vizier's son. He will soon be coming out of the baths; those officers and soldiers will escort him to the palace, where the Sultan's daughter is waiting for him.'

Aladdin's mother was very upset to hear this. She returned home with a heavy heart, not knowing how to break the alarming news to her son.

'My child,' said she, as soon as she entered the house, 'I have some bad news. I am afraid it will distress you.'

'What is it, Mother?' Aladdin asked impatiently.

'The Sultan has broken his promise to you, my child,' she answered. 'This very night the vizier's son is to marry the Princess. Oh, how I feared that the vizier would change the Sultan's mind! I told you he whispered something to him after he had accepted your proposal.'

'And how do you know,' Aladdin asked, 'that the vizier's son is to marry the Princess tonight?'

His mother described to him all that she had seen in the city: the lights and decorations, the soldiers and dignitaries waiting to escort the vizier's son on his bridal night. On hearing this, Aladdin was seized with a terrible rage; but he soon remembered the lamp and regained possession of himself.

'Upon your life, Mother,' he said, 'I do not think the vizier's son will be so happy tonight as he expects to be. Let us say no more about this. Get up and cook the dinner. Then I will go into my room and see what can be done. All will be well, I promise you.'

After dinner, Aladdin shut himself in his own room and locked the door. He then brought out the lamp and rubbed it, and at once the jinnee appeared.

'Ask what you will,' the jinnee said. 'I am your slave, and the slave of him who holds the lamp: I and the other slaves of the lamp will do your bidding.'

'Listen carefully,' Aladdin said. 'I asked the Sultan for his daughter and he promised that I should wed her after three months. He has now broken his promise and is marrying her to the vizier's son instead. The wedding takes place tonight. Now I command you, if you are indeed a trustworthy slave of the lamp, to take up the bride and bridegroom as soon as they have retired to sleep and bring them here in their bed. I will look after the rest myself.'

This was no sooner said than done, and the jinnee carried in the royal bed and set it down before Aladdin.

'Now take away this wretch,' Aladdin commanded, 'and lock him in the cellar.'

At once the jinnee carried away the vizier's son, laid him down in the cellar, and, breathing upon his body, left him paralyzed in every limb. Then he returned to Aladdin.

'Master, what else do you require?' he asked. 'Speak, and it shall be done.'

'Come again in the morning,' Aladdin answered.

'I hear and obey,' replied the jinnee; and so saying he vanished.

Aladdin could scarcely believe that all this had really happened, and that he was alone with the Princess whom he loved with a consuming passion.

'Adorable Princess,' he said, 'do not think that I have brought you here to harm you. Heaven forbid! I did this only to make sure that no one else would wed you, for your father, the Sultan, gave me his word that you would be my bride. Do not be alarmed; you will be safe here.'

When the Princess suddenly found herself in that dark and humble dwelling, and heard Aladdin's words, she was so terrified that she uttered not a word. Presently Aladdin laid himself down beside her on the bed, placing an unsheathed sword between them. But because of her fright the Princess did not sleep a wink all night. Nor did the vizier's son, who lay motionless on the floor of the filthy cellar.

Next morning the jinnee returned, without Aladdin's rubbing the lamp.

'Master,' he said, 'command, and I will gladly do your bidding.'

'Go,' cried Aladdin. 'Carry the bride and bride-groom back to the Sultan's palace.'

In a twinkling the jinnee did as Aladdin told him. He laid the vizier's son beside the Princess and took them both to the royal palace, so swiftly that the terrified couple could not see who had thus transported them. Scarcely had the jinnee set them down and disappeared than the Sultan came in to visit his daughter. This greatly distressed the vizier's son, for he was just beginning to feel warmer after his cold night in the cellar. However, he jumped to his feet, and put on his clothes.

The Sultan kissed his daughter and bade her good morning. But the girl looked dejectedly at him and said nothing. He questioned her again and again, and still she made no answer. At last he left her room in anger, and, taking himself off to the Queen, gave her an account of his daughter's strange behavior.

'Do not be harsh with her,' said the Queen,

wishing to calm him. 'In a short time she will return to her former ways and talk to people freely. I will go and speak to her myself.'

The Queen immediately went off to visit her daughter. She approached Badr-al-Budur and, kissing her between the eyes, wished her good morning. But the Princess said nothing.

'Something very odd must have happened to her to upset her so,' thought the Queen to herself. 'What grief is this, my daughter?' she asked. 'Tell me what has happened. Here I am, wishing you good morning, and you do not even return my greeting.'

'Do not be angry with me, Mother,' said the Princess, raising her head, 'but pardon the disrespect I have shown you. Look what a miserable night I passed! Scarcely had we gone to bed, when someone came – we could not see who he was – and carried us away, bed and all, to a damp, dark, and dirty place.'

Badr-al-Budur told her mother all that had passed during the night: how her husband had been taken away from her and replaced by another young man who lay beside her with a sword between them.

'Then, this morning,' she continued, 'the person who took us away returned and brought us back to this very room. As soon as he had set us down and gone, my father entered; but such was my terror at that moment that I had neither heart nor tongue to speak to him. If, for this reason, I have incurred his anger, I beg you to explain to him what has happened, so that he should not blame but pardon me for my offense.'

'Dear child!' exclaimed the Queen. 'Take care not to tell this story to anyone else. They will say the Sultan's daughter has gone mad. You were wise not to tell your father of all this. Say nothing about it to him, I warn you.'

'But, Mother, I am not mad,' the Princess replied. 'I have told you nothing but the truth. If you do not believe me, ask my husband.'

'Get up, child,' said the Queen, 'and drive this wild fantasy out of your head. Put on your clothes and go and watch the festivities that are being held all over the city in your honor. Listen to the drums and the singing; and look at the decorations, all celebrating your happy marriage.'

The Queen called her attendants, who dressed the Princess and combed her hair. Then, returning to the Sultan, she told him that Badr-al-Budur had had dreams and nightmares, and begged him not to be angry with her.

Next she sent in secret for the vizier's son and questioned him. 'Your Majesty, I know nothing of what you say,' he answered; for he was afraid lest he should lose his bride. The Queen was now convinced that the Princess was suffering from a nightmare or some unfortunate illusion.

The festivities continued all day, with dancers and singers performing in the palace to the accompaniment of all kinds of music. The Queen, the vizier, and the vizier's son did their best to keep the merriment afoot, to cheer the bride, and to dispel her gloom. But for all their efforts she remained silent and thoughtful, brooding over the happenings of the previous night. True, the vizier's son had suffered even more than she. But he denied it all, dreading that he might lose the honor that had been given him; especially since everyone envied him his luck in marrying a girl so noble and so fair as the Princess.

Aladdin went out that day and watched the rejoicings in the city and the palace with laughter in his heart, particularly when he heard the people speak of the distinction that the vizier's son had gained, and how fortunate he was to have become the Sultan's son-in-law.

'Poor fools!' he thought to himself. 'If only you knew what happened to him last night!'

In the evening he went into his room and rubbed the lamp. When the jinnee came he ordered him to bring the Sultan's daughter and her bridegroom, as on the previous night. The slave of the lamp vanished, and returned almost at once with the couple in the royal bed. Then he carried the vizier's son to the cellar, where he left him petrified with fear. Aladdin placed the sword between himself and the Princess and slept by her side. In the morning the jinnee brought back the husband and returned the bed to the palace. Aladdin was delighted with the progress of his plan.

When the Sultan woke up, his first thought was

to go to his daughter to see if she would act as on the day before. He dressed at once and went off to Badr-al-Budur's room. On hearing the door open, the vizier's son hurriedly dressed himself, his ribs almost cracking with the cold, for the slave of the lamp had just brought them back to the palace. The Sultan went up to his daughter's bed, lifted the curtains, and, kissing her on the cheek, wished her good morning. He asked how she was, but instead of answering she frowned and stared sullenly at him; for she was now desperately bewildered and upset. Her silence once again provoked the Sultan, who immediately sensed that she was hiding something from him.

'What has come over you, my girl?' he cried, drawing his sword. 'Tell me the truth, or I will cut off your head. Is this the respect you owe me? I speak to you, and you do not answer a single word.'

The Princess was terrified to see her father brandishing his sword over her.

'Do not be angry with me, I beg you,' she replied, lifting her head from the pillow. 'When you have heard what I have suffered these last two nights, you will excuse and pity me; for I have always known you as a most loving father.'

She then told the Sultan all that had happened.

'And now, Father,' she added, 'if you wish to confirm what I have said, ask my husband. He will tell you everything. I do not know what they did to him when they took him away, or where they put him.'

Moved by his daughter's words, the Sultan sheathed his sword and kissed her tenderly.

'My child,' he said, 'why did you not tell me of all this, so that I could have protected you from those terrors last night? But have no fear; get up, and dismiss these unpleasant thoughts. Tonight I will post guards around your room, and you shall be safe from all dangers.'

He returned to his room and at once sent for the vizier.

'What do you think of this business?' he cried, as soon as the vizier presented himself. 'Perhaps your son has told you what happened to him and my daughter?'

'Your Majesty, I have not seen my son these two days,' the vizier answered.

The Sultan told him the Princess' story.

'Now go to your son,' he added, 'and find out the whole truth from him. My daughter may be so frightened that she does not really know what has happened; though, for my part, I am inclined to believe her.'

The vizier called his son and asked him if what the Sultan had said was true or not.

'Heaven forbid that the Princess should tell a lie,' the young man answered. 'All that she says is true. These last two nights have been a nightmare for us both. What happened to me was even worse. I was locked up all night in a dark, frightful cellar, where I almost perished with cold.'

And he told him the story in all its details.

'I now beg you, Father,' he concluded, 'to speak to the Sultan and ask him to release me from this marriage. I know it is a great honor to be the Sultan's son-in-law, especially as I am so deeply in love with the Princess. But I cannot endure again what I went through these last two nights.'

The vizier was profoundly shocked to hear this, for his fondest wish had been to marry his son to the Sultan's daughter and thus make a prince of him.

'Be patient a little, my son,' he said. 'Let us see what happens tonight. We will post guards around your chamber. Do not so rashly cast away this great honor; no one else has attained it.'

The vizier left his son and, returning to the Sultan, informed him that the Princess' story was true.

'Then here and now,' rejoined the Sultan, 'I declare the marriage null and void.' And he gave orders that the rejoicings should cease and the marriage be dissolved.

The people of the city were amazed at the sudden change, especially when they saw the vizier and his son come out of the palace with forlorn and angry looks. They began to ask what had happened and why the marriage had been broken off. But nobody knew the secret except Aladdin, who was full of glee at the strange proceedings.

Now, the Sultan had forgotten the promise he had given Aladdin's mother. When the three months elapsed, Aladdin sent her to demand fulfillment. She went off to the palace, and as soon as she entered the audience hall the Sultan recognized her.

'Here comes the woman who presented me with the jewels,' said the Sultan, and after she had kissed the ground and wished him everlasting glory he asked her what she wanted.

'Your Majesty,' she said, 'the three months after which you promised to wed your daughter, the Princess, to my son, Aladdin, are up.'

The Sultan was at a loss what to answer, for it was plain that the woman was among the humblest of his subjects. Yet the present she had brought him was indeed beyond price.

'What do you suggest now?' he asked the vizier in a whisper. 'It is perfectly true that I made her such a promise. But they are such humble folk!'

The vizier, stung with envy, thought to himself, 'How can such a wretch marry the Princess, and my son be robbed of the honor?'

'Your Majesty,' he replied, 'that is no difficult thing. We must rebuff this stranger; for it scarcely befits your station to give away your daughter to an unknown upstart.'

'But how can we get rid of him?' rejoined the Sultan. 'I gave him my pledge, and a sultan's pledge must never be broken.'

'I suggest,' said the vizier, 'that you demand of him forty dishes of pure gold filled with jewels like the ones he has already sent you; the dishes to be carried in by forty slave girls, attended by forty slaves.'

'Well spoken, vizier!' replied the Sultan. 'That is something he can never do; in this way we shall once and for all be rid of him.'

The Sultan then turned to Aladdin's mother.

'Go to your son,' he said, 'and tell him that I stand by my promise. The marriage will take place when he has sent a fitting present for my daughter. I will require of him forty dishes of pure gold filled with the same kind of jewels as those you brought me, together with forty slave girls to carry them, and forty slaves. If your son can provide this gift, my daughter shall be his.'

Aladdin's mother left the royal presence in silence, and set out for home crestfallen. 'Where will my poor boy get all those plates and jewels?' she asked herself. 'Even if he returns to the treasure house and strips the magic trees of their jewels – not that I really believe that he can do this, but suppose he does – where in heaven's name are the forty girls and forty slaves to come from?'

Deep in these reflections, the old woman trudged on until she reached her house, where Aladdin was waiting.

'My child,' she said, as soon as she entered, 'did I not tell you to give up all thought of the Princess? Did I not warn you that such a thing was impossible for people like us?'

'Tell me what happened,' Aladdin demanded.

'The Sultan received me very kindly,' she replied, 'and I believe he was well disposed toward you. But your enemy is that odious vizier. When I had spoken to the Sultan and reminded him of his promise, he consulted his vizier, who whispered to him in secret. After that the Sultan gave me his answer.'

And she told Aladdin of the present that the Sultan had demanded.

'My child,' she added, 'the Sultan expects your answer now. But I think there is no answer we can give him.'

'So that is what you think, Mother,' Aladdin replied, laughing. 'You think it is impossible. Rise up now and get us something to eat; then you will see the answer for yourself. Like you, the Sultan thought that his demand was beyond my power. In fact it is a trifle. Go, I say, and get the dinner ready. The rest you can leave to me.'

His mother went off to the market to buy the food she needed. Meanwhile, Aladdin entered his room, took the lamp, and rubbed it; and at once the jinnee appeared.

'Master,' he said, 'ask what you will.'

'The Sultan is now willing to give me his daughter,' Aladdin said. 'But I must send him forty dishes of pure gold, each ten pounds in weight, filled to the brim with jewels like those in the garden of the treasure house. The dishes must be carried by forty girls, with forty slaves to attend them. Go and bring me these without delay.'

'I hear and obey,' the jinnee replied.

The slave of the lamp vanished, and after a while returned with forty girls, each attended by a handsome slave; on their heads the girls bore dishes of pure gold full of priceless gems. The jinnee led them before his master and asked if there was any other service he could render.

'Nothing at present,' Aladdin answered.

The jinnee disappeared again. In time Aladdin's mother returned from the market and was much amazed to see the house crowded with so many slaves.

'Could all this be the work of the lamp?' she exclaimed. 'Heaven preserve it for my boy!'

Before she had time to take off her veil, Aladdin said, 'Mother, there is not one moment to be lost. Take the Sultan the present he has asked for. Go to him now, so that he may realize I can give him all he wants and more besides.'

Aladdin opened the door and the girls and slaves marched out in pairs. When the passers-by saw this wondrous spectacle they stopped and marveled at the beauty of the girls, who were dressed in robes woven of gold and studded with jewels. They gazed at the dishes, too, and saw that they outshone the sun in their sparkling brilliance. Each dish was covered with a kerchief embroidered in gold and sewn with precious pearls.

Aladdin's mother led the long procession, and as it passed from street to street the people crowded around, agog with wonder and exclamations. At last the procession came to the palace and wound its way into the courtyard. The commanders and chamberlains marveled greatly at the sight, for never in all their lives had they seen anything like it. They were astounded by the magnificent robes the girls were wearing, and the dishes upon their heads, which glowed with such fiery radiance that they could scarcely open their eyes to look at them.

The courtiers went and informed the Sultan, who at once ordered the procession to be brought in. Aladdin's mother led them into his presence, and they all solemnly saluted the Sultan and called down blessings upon him. Then they set down their plates, lifted the covers, and stood upright with their arms crossed over their breasts. The Sultan was filled with wonderment at the rare elegance of the girls, whose beauty beggared description. He was dumbfounded when he saw the golden dishes brimful with dazzling gems, and was even more bewildered that all this could have happened in such a short time.

'What do you say now?' said the Sultan in a whisper, turning to the vizier. 'What shall be said of a man who can produce such riches in so short a time? Does he not deserve to be the Sultan's son-in-law, and take the Sultan's daughter for his bride?'

Now, the vizier was even more amazed than the Sultan at this prodigious wealth; but envy got the better of him. 'Your Majesty,' he cunningly replied, 'not all the treasures of the world are equal to the Princess' fingernail. Surely you overrate this gift in comparison with your daughter.' But the Sultan ignored the vizier's remark.

'Go to your son,' he said to Aladdin's mother, 'and tell him that I stand by my promise: my daughter shall be his bride. Tell him to come to the palace, so that I may meet him. He shall be received with the utmost honor and consideration. The wedding shall begin this very night; only, as I told you, let him come here without delay.'

Scarcely believing her ears, Aladdin's mother ran home swiftly as the wind to give the news to her son. The Sultan dismissed his court and ordered the slave girls to be brought in with the dishes to the Princess' room. The Princess marveled at the size of the jewels and the beauty of the slave girls, and was delighted to know that all this had been sent to her by her new husband. Her father, too, rejoiced to see her so happy and no longer cast down with gloom.

'Are you pleased with this present, my daughter?' he asked. 'I am sure that this young man will prove a better husband than the vizier's son. I hope you will be happy with him.'

So much for the Sultan. As for Aladdin, when he saw his mother enter the house beaming with joy, he knew that her mission had been successful.

'Rejoice, my boy,' she cried. 'You have gained your wish. The Sultan has accepted your present, and the Princess is to be your bride. Tonight the wedding festivities will begin. The Sultan is proclaiming you before the whole world as his son-in-law, and desires that you should call on him without delay.'

Aladdin kissed his mother's hand and thanked her with all his heart. Then he returned to his room, took up the lamp, and rubbed it. At once the jinnee appeared.

'I am here,' he said. 'Ask what you will.'

'Slave of the lamp,' said Aladdin, 'I order you to take me to a bath more magnificent than any in the world; also to bring me a splendid regal suit such as no king has ever worn.'

'I hear and obey,' the jinnee replied.

So saying, he took Aladdin upon his shoulder and in a twinkling brought him to a bath such as neither king nor emperor ever saw. It was made of agate and alabaster, and adorned with wondrous paintings that dazzled the eye. No mortal troubled the peace of that white vault. The slave of the lamp led him into an inner hall, thickly studded with jewels and precious stones, and there he was received and washed by a jinnee in human shape. After his bath, Aladdin was led back into the outer vault, where, instead of his former clothes, he found a magnificent regal suit. Cool drinks were brought to him, and coffee flavored with amber; and when he had refreshed himself, there came into the hall a train of slaves who perfumed him and dressed him in his sumptuous robes.

Aladdin, as you know, was the son of a poor tailor; yet anyone who saw him now would have taken him for some illustrious prince. As soon as he was dressed, the jinnee appeared again and carried him home.

'Master,' said the jinnee, 'is there anything else that you require?'

'Yes,' Aladdin replied. 'I want you to bring me a retinue of four dozen slaves, two dozen to ride before me and two dozen to ride behind me, complete with livery, horses, and weapons. Both slaves and horses must be arrayed in the finest and the best. After that, bring me a thoroughbred steed worthy of an emperor's stable, with trappings all of gold studded with rich jewels. You must also bring me forty-eight thousand gold pieces, a thousand with each slave. Do not delay; all these must be ready before I go to the Sultan. Lastly, be careful to select twelve girls of incomparable beauty, dressed in the most exquisite clothes, to accompany my mother to the royal palace; and let each girl bring with her a robe that would do credit to a queen.'

'I hear and obey,' the jinnee replied.

He vanished, and in the twinkling of an eye returned with everything Aladdin had asked for. In his hand he held the bridle of a horse unrivaled among all the Arabian steeds for beauty, with trappings of the finest cloth of gold. Aladdin at once called his mother and gave her charge of the twelve girls; he also gave her a robe to put on when she went with her attendants to the royal palace. Then he sent one of the slaves to see whether the Sultan was ready to receive him. The slave departed, and in a flash returned.

'Master,' he said, 'the Sultan is waiting for you.'

Aladdin mounted his horse, while his attendants mounted before and behind him. As they rode they scattered handfuls of gold among the crowd. And so handsome and radiant did Aladdin look that he would have put to shame the greatest of princes.

All this was due to the power of the lamp; for whoever possessed it acquired beauty, wealth, and all knowledge. The people marveled at Aladdin's generosity; they were amazed at his good looks, his politeness, and his noble bearing. No one envied him; they all said he deserved his good luck.

Meanwhile the Sultan had assembled the great ones of his kingdom to inform them of the intended marriage. He told them to wait for Aladdin's arrival and to go out in a body to receive him. He also summoned the viziers and the chamberlains, the nabobs and the commanders of the army; and they all stood waiting for Aladdin at the gates of the palace. Presently Aladdin arrived and would have dismounted at the entrance; but one of the commanders, whom the Sultan had stationed there for the purpose, hastened to prevent him.

'Sir,' he said, 'it is His Majesty's wish that you should enter riding and dismount at the door of the audience hall.'

The courtiers walked before him, and when he had reached the audience hall some came forward to hold his horse's stirrup, others to support him on either side, while yet others took him by the hand and helped him to dismount. The commanders and dignitaries ushered him into the hall, and as soon as he approached the throne and was about to kneel on the carpet the Sultan stepped forward, took him in his arms, and made him sit down on his right. Aladdin exchanged greetings with him and wished him long life and everlasting glory.

'Your Majesty,' he said, 'you have been graciously pleased to give me your daughter in marriage, although, being the humblest of your subjects, I am unworthy of so great an honor. Great Sultan, I lack the words to thank you for this signal favor. I beg Your Majesty to grant me a plot of land where I can build a palace worthy of Princess Badr-al-Budur.'

The Sultan was greatly astonished when he saw Aladdin dressed in such splendor. He looked intently at him, and then at the tall and handsome slaves who stood around him. He was even more amazed when Aladdin's mother made her entrance, radiant as a queen in her costly robes and surrounded by the twelve graceful girls, who were attending her with the utmost dignity and respect. He marveled, too, at Aladdin's eloquence and cultured speech; and so did all the others present in the audience hall except the vizier, who almost perished with envy. Having listened to Aladdin's words and observed his magnificence and modest bearing, the Sultan again took him in his arms.

'It is a great pity, my son,' he said, 'that we have not been brought together before this.'

He ordered the musicians to start playing; then he took Aladdin by the hand and led him into the palace hall, where a wedding feast had been prepared. The Sultan sat down and made Aladdin sit on his right. The viziers, dignitaries, and noblemen also took their seats, each according to his rank. Music filled the air, and all the palace echoed with the sound of great rejoicing. The Sultan spoke to Aladdin and jested with him, while Aladdin replied with gallantry and wit, as though he had grown up in a royal palace and all his life kept company with kings. And the longer the Sultan talked to him, the more impressed he became with his accomplishments.

When they had finished eating, and the tables were removed, the Sultan ordered judges and witnesses to be brought in. They came, and duly wrote the marriage contract for Aladdin and the Princess. Then Aladdin got up and begged leave to go; but the Sultan prevented him.

'Where are you going, my son?' he cried. 'All the wedding guests are here and the feast is not yet finished.'

'Your Majesty,' Aladdin replied, 'I wish to build the Princess a palace befitting her high station. I cannot take her as my wife until I have done that. I hope that the palace will be ready in the shortest possible time. Eager as I am to be with the Princess, my duty prompts me to do this first, in proof of the great love I bear her.'

'Take whatever land you like, my son,' the Sultan said. 'It is for you to choose. But to my mind it would be best to build it here, on the great square in front of my palace.'

'I could wish for nothing better,' Aladdin replied, 'than to be so near Your Majesty.'

With that he took leave of the Sultan and, mounting his horse, returned home amid the joyful shouts of the people.

There he went into his room and rubbed the lamp.

'Master, ask what you will,' said the jinnee, as he appeared before him.

'I have an important task to set you,' Aladdin replied. 'I wish you to build me, with the least possible delay, a palace in front of the Sultan's; a marvel of a building, the like of which no king has ever seen. Let it be furnished royally and fitted with every comfort.'

'I hear and obey,' the jinnee answered.

He disappeared and, just before daybreak, returned to Aladdin, saying, 'Master, the task is accomplished. Rise and look upon your palace.'

Aladdin got up, and in the twinkling of an eye the slave of the lamp carried him away to the palace. When Aladdin saw it he was dumbfounded with wonder; it was all built of jasper and marble mosaics. The jinnee conducted him into a treasury heaped with all manner of gold and silver and precious stones beyond count or value. He then led him into the dining hall, where he saw plates and ewers, cups and spoons and basins, all of gold and silver. He next took him to the kitchen, and there he saw the cooks with their pots and utensils, also of gold and silver. From there he led him into another room, which he found stacked with coffers containing rich and wondrous garments, Chinese and Indian silks embroidered with gold, and thick brocades. After that he ushered him into several other rooms, full of treasures beyond description, and finally took him into the stables, where he saw thoroughbred horses whose like no king ever possessed. In an adjoining storeroom lay costly saddles and bridles wrought with pearls and rich jewels. All this had been accomplished in one night.

Aladdin was bewildered and amazed at these marvels, which were beyond the dream of kings. The palace was thronged with slaves and serving girls of exquisite beauty. But the most wondrous thing of all was the dome of the building, which was pierced with four and twenty windows encrusted with emeralds, rubies, and other precious stones. At Aladdin's request, one of the windows had not been properly finished, for he wished to challenge the Sultan to complete it. Aladdin was overjoyed at the splendor of all he saw.

'There is only one thing lacking, which I forgot to mention,' he said, turning to the slave of the lamp.

'Ask,' the jinnee replied, 'and it shall be done.'

'I require a carpet of rich brocade, woven with

thread of gold,' said Aladdin. 'It must be stretched from this palace to the Sultan's so that the Princess may walk upon it without her feet touching the ground.'

The jinnee vanished, and almost at once returned.

'Master, your request is granted,' he said.

He took Aladdin and showed it to him: a wonder of a carpet, stretching from his palace to the Sultan's. Then the jinnee carried him home.

When the Sultan woke that morning, he opened the window of his bedroom and looked out. In front of his palace he saw a building. He rubbed his eyes, opened them wide, and looked again. The building was still there, a towering edifice of astonishing beauty, with a carpet stretched from its threshold to the doorstep of his own palace. The doorkeepers and everyone else who saw it were no less astounded. At that moment the vizier entered the Sultan's apartment, and he too was utterly amazed to see the new palace and the carpet.

'Heavens!' they cried together. 'No king on earth could ever build the like of that palace!'

'Now are you convinced that Aladdin deserves to be my daughter's husband?' said the Sultan, turning to his minister.

'Your Majesty,' the vizier answered, 'nothing short of magic could have produced that edifice. Not the richest man alive could build such a palace in one night.'

'I marvel at you,' the Sultan cried. 'You seem to think nothing but ill of Aladdin. Clearly you are jealous of him. You were present yourself when I gave him this land to erect a palace for my daughter. The man who could present a gift of such jewels can surely build a palace in one night.'

Realizing that the Sultan loved Aladdin too well to be aroused against him, the vizier held his peace and said no more.

As for Aladdin, when he felt that the time was ripe to present himself at the royal palace, he rubbed the lamp and said to the jinnee, 'I must now go to the Sultan's court; today is the wedding banquet. I want you to bring me ten thousand pieces of gold.'

The jinnee vanished and, in a twinkling returned with ten thousand gold pieces. Aladdin mounted his horse, and his slaves rode before and behind him. All along the way he scattered gold among the people, who now made him their idol on account of his generosity. As soon as he reached the palace, the courtiers and officers of the guard hurried to inform the Sultan of his arrival. The Sultan went out to receive him; he took him by the hand, led him into the hall, and seated him on his right. The entire city was decorated, and in the palace performers sang and made music.

Orders were now given by the Sultan for the banquet to begin. He sat at a table with Aladdin and all the courtiers, and they ate and drank until they were satisfied. Nor was the merriment confined to the royal palace; all the people of the kingdom, great and small alike, rejoiced on this happy occasion. Viceroys and governors had come from the remotest provinces to see the wedding and the nuptial celebrations.

Deep in his heart, the Sultan marveled at Aladdin's mother, how she had come to him in tattered clothes, while her son was master of such extraordinary riches. And when the guests saw Aladdin's palace, they were amazed that such a dwelling could have been built in one night.

When the banquet drew to an end, Aladdin rose and took leave of the Sultan. He mounted his horse and, escorted by his servants, rode over to his own palace to prepare himself for his meeting with the bride. As he rode he threw handfuls of gold to right and left amid the joyful blessings of the people, and on reaching his house alighted and took his seat in the audience hall. Cool drinks were brought to him, and after he had refreshed himself he ordered the servants and the slave girls, and everyone else in the palace, to make ready to receive his bride that evening.

In the cool of the afternoon, when the heat of the sun had abated, the Sultan ordered his captains and ministers to go down and take their places in the parade ground opposite his court. They all went down, including the Sultan; and Aladdin presently joined them, riding on a horse unequaled among the Arabian steeds for beauty. He galloped and sported around the square, excelling in his display of horsemanship. The Princess watched him from a window; she was captivated by his good looks and riding skill, and fell in love with him at sight. When all the cavaliers had finished their riding display, the Sultan returned to his palace and Aladdin to his.

In the evening the ministers and high officials called on Aladdin and took him in great procession to the royal baths. There he bathed and perfumed himself, then changed into even more magnificent clothes and rode home escorted by officers and soldiers. Four ministers walked about him with unsheathed swords, while all the townsfolk, natives and foreigners alike, marched ahead with candles and drums, pipes, and all manner of musical instruments. Reaching the palace, he dismounted and sat down with his attendants. The slaves brought cakes and sweetmeats and served drinks to countless men and women who had joined the procession. Then, at Aladdin's orders, the slaves went out to the palace gate and scattered gold among the people.

Meanwhile, on returning from the square, the Sultan had ordered his household to take the Princess to Aladdin's palace. The soldiers and courtiers immediately mounted; the servants and slave girls went out with lighted candles, and the Princess was brought in splendid procession to her husband's palace. Aladdin's mother walked by her side; in front marched the wives of ministers, noblemen, and courtiers, while in her train followed all the slave girls whom Aladdin had given her, each carrying a torch set into a golden candlestick encrusted with gems. They took her up to her room, accompanied by Aladdin's mother.

Presently Aladdin entered the chamber; he lifted the bridal veil, and his mother gazed in wonderment upon the Princess' loveliness and beauty. She also marveled at the bridal chamber, all wrought in gold and jewels, and at its golden chandelier, studded with emeralds and rubies. Nor was the Princess less astonished than Aladdin's mother at the magnificence of the palace.

A table was brought in and they feasted and made merry, while eighty slave girls, each holding a musical instrument, plucked the strings and played enchanting tunes. The Princess was so thrilled with the music that she stopped eating and listened with rapt attention. Aladdin plied her with wine, and the two rejoiced in each other's love.

In the morning Aladdin got up and dressed himself in a magnificent suit that his chief footman had prepared for him. Then he ordered the slaves to saddle his horses and rode with numerous escorts to the royal palace. The Sultan at once rose to receive him and, after embracing him as though he were his own son, seated him on his right. The Sultan and all the courtiers congratulated him and wished him joy. Breakfast was then served, and when they had finished eating, Aladdin turned to the Sultan and said, 'Sir, would Your Majesty honor me with your presence at lunch today with the Princess? Let Your Majesty be accompanied by all your ministers and the nobles of your kingdom.'

The Sultan gladly accepted. He ordered his courtiers to follow him and rode over with Aladdin to his palace. When he entered he marveled at the edifice, the stones of which were all of jasper and agate; he was dazed at the sight of such luxury, wealth, and splendor.

'What do you say now?' he exclaimed, turning to the vizier. 'Have you ever seen anything like this in all your life? Has the greatest emperor in the world such wealth and gold and jewels as can be seen in this palace?'

'Your Majesty,' the vizier replied, 'this miracle is beyond the power of mortal kings. Not all the people of the world could build a palace like this; no masons are to be found who can do such work. As I told Your Majesty before, only magic would have brought it into being.'

But the Sultan replied, 'Enough, vizier. I know why you are telling me this.'

The Sultan now came under the lofty dome of the palace, and his amazement knew no bounds when he saw that all the windows and lattices were made of emeralds, rubies, and other precious stones. He walked around and around, bewildered at the extravagant marvels, and presently caught sight of the window that Aladdin had deliberately left unfinished.

'Alas, poor window, you are unfinished!' observed the Sultan. And, turning to the vizier, he asked, 'Do you know why that window and its lattices have not been properly completed?'

'Perhaps because Your Majesty hurried Aladdin over the wedding,' the vizier replied. 'He may not have had time enough to complete it.'

Aladdin, who had meanwhile gone to inform his bride of her father's arrival, now returned, and the Sultan addressed the same question to him.

'Your Majesty,' he replied, 'the wedding took place at such short notice that the masons had no time to finish the work.'

'Then I would like to finish it myself,' said the Sultan.

'Heaven grant Your Majesty everlasting glory!' Aladdin cried. 'May it stand as a memorial to you in your daughter's palace!'

The Sultan at once sent for jewelers and goldsmiths and ordered his lieutenants to give them all the gold and jewels they required out of his treasury. The jewelers and goldsmiths presented themselves before the Sultan, and he ordered them to finish the ornamentation.

While this was going forward, the Princess came out to meet her father. He noticed how happy she was, and took her into his arms and kissed her; then he went with her to her room, followed by all his courtiers. It was now lunchtime; one table had been prepared for the Sultan, the Princess, and Aladdin, and another for the vizier, the officers of state, the high dignitaries, the chamberlains, the nabobs, and the captains of the army. The Sultan sat between his daughter and his son-in-law, and as he ate he marveled at the delicacy of the meats and the excellence of the dishes. Before him stood a troupe of eighty radiant girls, who plucked the strings of their instruments and made such sweet music as could not be heard even in the courts of kings and emperors. Wine flowed freely; and when all had eaten and drunk, they repaired to an adjoining chamber, where they were served with fruits and sweetmeats.

Then the Sultan rose to inspect the jewelers' work, and to see how it compared with the workmanship of the palace. He went up to the unfinished window, but was disappointed to find that there was a great difference, and that his workers lacked the art to match the perfection of the whole. The jewelers informed him that they had brought all the gems they could find in his treasury, and that they needed more. He ordered that the great imperial treasury be opened and that they should be given all they required; if that was not enough, they were to use the jewels that Aladdin had sent him. The jewelers did as the Sultan had directed, but found that all those gems were not sufficient to ornament one half of the lattice. The Sultan next commanded that all the precious stones that could be found in the houses of the viziers and rich notables should be taken. The jewelers took all of these and worked with them, but still they needed more.

Next morning Aladdin went up to the jewelers and, finding that they had not finished even half the lattice, told them to undo their work and restore the gems to their owners. The jewelers did so, and went to inform the Sultan of Aladdin's instructions.

'What did he say to you?' the Sultan asked. 'Why did he not let you finish the window? Why did he destroy what you had done?'

'We do not know, Your Majesty,' was their reply.

The Sultan called for his horse and rode at once to his son-in-law's palace.

Now, when Aladdin had dismissed the jewelers, he had entered his room and rubbed the lamp. The jinnee appeared before him, saying, 'Ask what you will, your slave is at your service.'

'I want you to complete the unfinished window,' Aladdin commanded.

'It shall be as you wish,' the jinnee replied.

He vanished, and after a short while returned.

'Master,' he said, 'the task is accomplished.'

Aladdin climbed up to the dome of the palace and saw that all its windows were now complete. While he was examining them his footman came in to inform him that the Sultan had come. Aladdin went down to receive him.

'Why did you do that, my son?' cried the Sultan as soon as he saw him. 'Why did you not let the jewelers complete the lattice, so that there would remain nothing amiss in your palace?'

'Great Sultan,' Aladdin replied, 'it was left unfinished at my request. I was not incapable of completing it myself; nor would I wish to receive Your Majesty in a palace where there was something missing. May it please Your Highness to come up and see if there is anything imperfect now.'

The Sultan mounted the stairs and went into the dome of the palace. He looked right and left, and was astonished to see that all the latticework was now complete.

'What an extraordinary feat, my son!' he exclaimed. 'In a single night you have finished a task that would have occupied the jewelers for months. Why, there cannot be anyone like you in the whole world!'

'Your Majesty,' Aladdin replied, 'your servant is unworthy of such praise.'

'My son,' the Sultan cried, 'you deserve all praise, because you have done that which no jeweler on earth could ever do.'

From that time on, Aladdin went out into the city every day, his slaves scattering gold before him as he rode. The hearts of all the people, old and young, were drawn to him on account of his good deeds, and his fame spread far and wide throughout the realm.

It also happened at that time that certain enemies marched against the Sultan, who gathered his armies and appointed Aladdin commander in chief. Aladdin led the troops to the battlefield, unsheathed his sword, and with extraordinary courage attacked the opposing forces. A mighty battle took place, in which the raiders were defeated and put to flight. Aladdin plundered their goods and belongings and returned in glorious triumph to the capital, which had been gaily decked to receive him. The Sultan came out to meet him; he congratulated him on his victory and took him into his arms amid the rejoicings of the people. He ordered the entire kingdom to be decorated in honor of the occasion. The soldiers and all the people now looked only to God in heaven and to Aladdin on earth. They loved him more than ever on account of his generosity and patriotism, his horsemanship and heroic courage. So much for Aladdin.

Now to return to the Moorish sorcerer. When he had left Aladdin to perish in the cave, he journeyed back to his own land and passed his days bemoaning the vain hardships he had endured to secure the lamp. It pained him to think how the long-sought morsel had flown out of his hand just when it had reached his mouth, and he cursed Aladdin in his rage.

'I am very glad,' he would sometimes say to himself, 'that the little wretch has perished under the ground. The lamp is still safe in the treasure house, and I may get it yet.'

One day he cast his magic sand to ascertain Aladdin's death and the exact position of the lamp.

He studied the resulting figures attentively, but he saw no lamp. Angrily he cast the sand a second time to confirm that the boy was dead, but he did not see him in the treasure house. His fury mounted when he learned that Aladdin was alive; he realized that he must have come up from the cave and gained possession of the lamp.

'I have suffered many hardships, and endured pains such as no other man could bear, on account of the lamp,' he thought to himself. 'Now this worthless boy has taken it. It is all too clear that if he has discovered its magic power, he must now be the wealthiest man on earth. I must seek to destroy him.'

He cast the sand once more and scanned the figures. He found that Aladdin was master of great riches, and that he was married to a princess. Mad with envy, he set out for China. After a long journey he reached the capital where Aladdin lived, and put up at a travelers' inn. There he heard the people talk of nothing but the magnificence of Aladdin's palace. When he had rested a little, he changed his clothes and went out for a walk in the streets of the city. Wherever he passed he heard tell of nothing but the beauty of Aladdin and his manly grace, his generosity and rare virtues. The magician went up to a man who was praising Aladdin in these terms and said, 'Tell me, my good friend, who is this man of whom you speak so highly?'

'Why, sir, you must be a stranger in these

parts,' came the reply. 'But even if you are, have you never heard of Prince Aladdin? His palace is one of the wonders of the world. How is it that you have never heard of it?'

'I would very much like to see the palace,' said the magician. 'Would you be so kind as to direct me to it? I am indeed a stranger in this city.'

'Why, gladly,' the man replied and, walking before the magician, brought him to Aladdin's palace.

The magician looked at the building and realized that it was the work of the enchanted lamp.

'Ah,' he thought to himself, 'I must dig a pit for this vile tailor's son who could never earn an evening's meal before. If fate allows it, I will destroy him utterly, and send his mother back to her spinning wheel.'

Eaten up with sorrow and envy, he returned to his lodging and took out his magic board. He cast the sand to find out where the lamp was hidden, and saw that it was in the palace and not on Aladdin's person.

'My task is easy now,' he cried with joy. 'I know a way of getting the lamp.'

He went off to a coppersmith and said to him, 'Make me a few copper lamps. I will pay you well if you finish them fast enough.'

'I hear and obey,' replied the coppersmith and set to work at once.

When they were finished, the magician paid him without haggling, took the lamps, and returned to his lodging. There he put them in a basket, and went about the streets and markets, crying, 'Who will exchange an old lamp for a new one?'

When the people heard his cry, they laughed at him.

'No doubt the man is mad,' they said to each other. 'Who would go around offering to change old lamps for new?'

A great crowd followed him, and the street urchins ran after him from place to place, shouting and laughing. But the magician took no notice of them and proceeded on his way until he found himself in front of Aladdin's palace. Here he began to shout at the top of his voice, while the children chanted back, 'Madman! Madman!' At last the Princess, who happened to be in the hall of the latticed dome, heard the noise in the street and ordered one of the maids to go and find out what it was all about.

The maid returned to the Princess and said, 'Your Highness, outside the gate there is an old man crying, "Who will exchange an old lamp for a new one?" Little boys are laughing at him.'

The Princess laughed, too, at this strange offer. Now, Aladdin had left the lamp in his room and forgotten to lock it up. One of the girls, who had chanced to see it there, said, 'Mistress, there is an old lamp in my master Aladdin's room. Let us take it down to the old man and see if he will really exchange it for a new one.'

'Fetch it to me, then,' said the Princess.

Badr-al-Budur knew nothing of the lamp or its magic powers, nor was she aware that it was this lamp that had brought Aladdin such vast wealth. She merely wished to see what sort of madness drove the magician to change old things for new.

The maid went up to Aladdin's room and returned with the lamp to her mistress, who then ordered a servant to go and exchange it for a new one. The servant gave the lamp to the Moor, took a new one in return, and carried it to the Princess. Badr-al-Budur examined it and, finding that it really was new, laughed at the old man's folly.

When the magician recognized the lamp he quickly hid it in the breast of his robe and flung his basket with all its contents to the crowd. He ran on and on until he came outside the city and reached the empty plains. Then he waited for the night and, when all was darkness, took out the lamp and rubbed it. At once the jinnee appeared before him.

'I am here, master,' he said; 'ask what you will.'

'Slave of the lamp,' the magician said, 'I order you to lift up Aladdin's palace with all its contents and to transport it, and me as well, to my own country in Africa. You know my native city; there you shall set it down, among the gardens.'

'I hear and obey,' the jinnee replied. 'Shut your eyes and open them and you shall find yourself in your own land with the palace.'

At once the thing was done. In a flash the

magician and Aladdin's palace, together with all that it contained, were carried off to Africa.

So much for the Moorish magician.

Now to return to the Sultan and Aladdin. When the Sultan got up next day he opened the window and looked out, as was his custom every day, in the direction of his daughter's palace. But he saw nothing there, only a vast, bare space as in the former days. He was greatly astonished and perplexed; he rubbed his eyes, opened them wide, and looked again. But he saw not a trace or vestige of the palace, and could not understand how or why it had vanished. He wrung his hands in despair and tears began to roll over his beard, for he did not know what had become of his daughter. At once he summoned the vizier; and when the vizier came in and saw the Sultan overcome with grief, he cried, 'Heaven preserve Your Majesty from all evil! Why do I see you so distressed?'

'Is it possible that you do not know the reason?' the Sultan asked.

'By my honor, I know nothing,' returned the vizier, 'nothing at all.'

'Then you have not looked in the direction of Aladdin's palace?' the Sultan cried.

'No,' the vizier answered.

'Since you know nothing about the matter,' groaned the Sultan, 'pray have a good look from the window and see where Aladdin's palace is.'

The vizier crossed over to the window and

looked out toward Aladdin's palace. He saw nothing there, neither palace nor anything else. Confounded at the mystery, he returned to the Sultan.

'Well,' said the Sultan, 'do you know now the reason for my grief?'

'Great Sultan,' the vizier answered, 'I have told Your Majesty time and time again that the palace and the whole affair were magic from beginning to end.'

'Where is Aladdin?' cried the Sultan, blazing with rage.

'Gone to the hunt,' the vizier replied.

The Sultan instantly ordered a troop of officers and guards to go and bring Aladdin before him, manacled and bound with chains. The officers and guards rode off on their mission, and before long met Aladdin.

'Pardon us, master,' they said. 'We are commanded by the Sultan to take you to him in chains. We beg you to excuse us; we are acting under royal orders, which we cannot disobey.'

Aladdin was dumbfounded at these words, for he could think of no possible reason.

'Good friend,' he said at last to the officers, 'do you know why the Sultan gave these orders? I know I am innocent; I have committed no crime against the Sultan or his realm.'

'Master,' they replied, 'we know nothing at all.'

'Then you must carry out your orders,' said Aladdin, dismounting. 'Obedience to the Sultan is binding on all his loyal subjects.'

The officers chained their captive and dragged him in fetters to the capital. When the citizens saw Aladdin treated in this way, they realized that he was going to be put to death. But since they all loved him, they crowded in the street and, arming themselves with clubs and weapons, pressed at his heels to find out what would happen to him.

The troops took Aladdin to the palace and informed the Sultan, who thereupon commanded the executioner to strike off his head. When the citizens learned of this order they locked up the gates of the palace and sent a warning to the Sultan, saying, 'This very hour we will pull down your dwelling over your head and the heads of all who are in it, if Aladdin comes to the slightest harm.'

The vizier went in and delivered the warning to the Sultan.

'Your Majesty,' he said, 'this order will be the end of us all. It would be far better to pardon Aladdin, or the consequences would be terrible indeed. Your subjects love Aladdin more than us.'

Meanwhile the executioner made ready to do his work. He had just bandaged Aladdin's eyes and walked around him three times, waiting for the final order, when the Sultan saw his subjects storming the palace and climbing over the walls to destroy it. At once he ordered the executioner to stay his hand, and bade the crier go out among the people and proclaim that the Sultan had spared Aladdin's life.

Freed from his fetters, Aladdin went up to the Sultan.

'Your Majesty,' he said, 'since you have been graciously pleased to spare my life, I beg you to tell me what I have done to earn your displeasure.'

'Traitor,' the Sultan exclaimed, 'do you dare pretend you know nothing of what has happened?' Then, turning to the vizier, he said, 'Take him, and let him see from the window where his palace is!'

The vizier led Aladdin to a window, and he looked out toward his palace. He found the site desolate and empty, with not a trace of any building upon it. He returned, utterly bewildered, to the Sultan.

'What did you see?' the Sultan asked. 'Where is your palace? And where is my daughter, my only child?'

'Great Sultan,' Aladdin answered, 'I know nothing of all this, nor do I know what has happened.'

'Listen, Aladdin,' the Sultan cried. 'I have released you only that you may go and investigate this mystery and seek out my daughter for me. Do not return without her. If you fail to bring her back, I swear by my life that I will cut off your head.'

'I hear and obey, Your Majesty,' Aladdin replied. 'Only grant me a delay of forty days. If I do not bring her to you by that time, cut off my head and do with me what you will.'

'Very well,' the Sultan said. 'I grant you the delay. But do not think you can escape my reach; for I will bring you back even if you are above the clouds.'

The people were glad to see Aladdin free. He came out of the palace pleased at his escape; but the disgrace of what had happened, and the triumphant glee of his enemies, caused him to hang his head. For two days he wandered sadly about the town, not knowing what he should do, while certain friends secretly brought him food and drink. Then he struck aimlessly into the desert and journeyed on until he came to a river. Thirsty and worn out, he knelt down upon the bank to wash and refresh himself. He took up the water in the hollow of his hands and began to rub between his fingers; and in so doing he rubbed the ring that the magician had given him. Thereupon a jinnee appeared, saying, 'I am here. Your slave stands before you. Ask what you will.'

Aladdin rejoiced at the sight of the jinnee.

'Slave of the ring,' he cried, 'bring me back my wife and my palace with all its contents.'

'Master,' the jinnee replied, 'that is beyond my power, for it concerns only the slave of the lamp.'

'Very well,' Aladdin said. 'Since you cannot do this, take me away and set me down beside my palace, wherever it may be.'

'I hear and obey, master.'

So saying, the jinnee carried him up, and in the twinkling of an eye set him down beside his palace in Morocco, in front of his wife's room. Night had fallen; and as he looked at his palace his cares and sorrows left him. He prayed, after he had given up all hope, to be united with his wife again. As he had had no sleep for four days on account of his anxiety and grief, he stretched himself out by the palace and slept under a tree; for, as I have told you, the palace stood among the gardens of Africa, outside a town.

Thus, despite the anxious thoughts that troubled him, he slept soundly under the tree until daybreak, when he awoke to the singing of birds. He got up and walked down to a nearby river that flowed into the town, washed his hands and face, and said his prayers. Then he returned and sat down under the window of the Princess' room.

The Princess, very distressed at being separated from her husband and father, neither ate nor drank, and passed her days and nights weeping. As luck would have it, however, on that morning, when one of the maids came in to dress the Princess, she opened the window to cheer her mistress with the delightful view and saw Aladdin, her master, sitting below.

'Mistress, mistress!' she exclaimed. 'There is my master Aladdin, sitting below!'

The Princess rushed to the window, and husband and wife recognized each other in a transport of joy.

'Come up, quickly!' the Princess shouted. 'Enter by the secret door. The magician is not here now.'

Her maid ran down and opened a secret door, by which Aladdin went in to his wife's room. Laughing and crying, they fell into each other's arms.

'Before all else, Badr-al-Budur,' said Aladdin, when they had both sat down, 'tell me what became of that copper lamp that I left in my room when I went out hunting.'

'Alas, my love!' sighed the Princess. 'That lamp and nothing else was the cause of our ruin.'

'Tell me everything.'

Badr-al-Budur recounted to him all that had happened since the day she exchanged the old lamp for a new one.

'Next morning,' she said, 'we suddenly found ourselves in this country. And the man who cheated us told me that it was all done by his witchcraft and the power of the lamp; that he was a Moor from Africa and that we were now in his native city.'

'What does the scoundrel intend to do with you?' asked Aladdin, when the Princess had finished speaking. 'What does he say to you? What does he want of you?'

'He comes to me once every day,' she replied, 'and tries to win my heart. He wants me to forget you and to take *him* for my husband. He says that the Sultan has cut off your head, that you come of a poor family, and that you owe your wealth to him. He tries to endear himself to me, but gets nothing in return except silence and tears. He has never heard a kind word from me.'

'Now tell me where he keeps the lamp.'

'He always carries it with him,' the Princess replied, 'and never parts from it even for a moment. But he once drew it from his robe and showed it to me.'

Aladdin was very glad to hear this.

'Listen to me, Badr-al-Budur,' he said. 'I will leave the palace now, and return in a disguise. Do not be alarmed when you see me. Post one of the maids at the secret door, so that she may let me in. I have hit upon a plan to destroy this foul magician.'

Aladdin set off in the direction of the city, and presently met a peasant on the way.

'Good friend,' he said, 'take my clothes and give me yours.'

The peasant refused; so Aladdin took hold of him, forced him to cast off his clothes, put them on himself, and gave him his own costly robes in return. Then he walked on to the city and made his way to the perfume sellers' market, where he bought a powerful drug.

Returning to the palace, he went in by the secret door to the Princess' room.

'Listen, now,' he said to his wife. 'I want you to put on your finest robes and jewels and to look your radiant self again. When the magician comes, give him a joyful welcome and receive him with a smiling face. Invite him to dine with you; pretend you have forgotten your husband and your father, and you are in love with him. Ask him for red wine, and drink his health with a show of merriment. When you have given him two or three glasses, drop this powder into his cup and fill it to the brim with wine. As soon as he has drunk it off, he will fall over on his back like a dead man.'

'That will be difficult,' the Princess replied. 'Yet it must be done if we are to rid ourselves of the monster. To kill such a man is certainly a good deed.'

Then Aladdin ate and drank with the Princess, and when he had satisfied his hunger he got up and quickly left the palace.

The Princess sent for her maid, who combed her hair, perfumed her, and dressed her in her finest garments. By and by, the Moor came in. He was delighted to see her so changed, and was agreeably surprised when she received him with a welcoming smile. She took him by the hand and seated him by her side.

'If you wish, sir,' she said in a tender voice, 'come to my room tonight and we will dine together. I have had my fill of grief; and were I to sit mourning for a thousand years, Aladdin would never come back from the grave. I have thought about what you told me yesterday, and do believe that my father may well have killed him in his sorrow at being parted from me. Therefore you must not be surprised to see me changed. Pray let us meet tonight, that we may have dinner and drink a little wine together. I would particularly like to taste your African wine; perhaps it is better than ours. I have here some wine from our own country, but would much prefer to try some of yours.'

Taken in by the affectionate regard that the Princess displayed toward him, the magician concluded that she had given up all hope of Aladdin. Therefore he rejoiced and said, 'My dear, I will gladly obey your every wish. I have in my house a cask of African wine, which I have stored deep under the earth these eight years. I will now go and fetch from it sufficient for our needs, and return to you without delay.'

But to coax him more and more, the Princess replied, 'Do not leave me alone, dearest. Send one of your servants for the wine, and sit here by my side, that I may cheer myself with your company.'

'Dear mistress,' the magician answered, 'no one knows where the cask is hidden but myself. I will not be long.'

So saying, he went out and after a little while returned with a flaskful of the wine.

'Dearest,' said the Princess when he entered, 'you have tired yourself on my account.'

'Not at all, my love,' the magician replied. 'It is an honor for me to serve you.'

The Princess sat beside him at the table, and the two ate together. She asked for a drink, and her maid filled her cup and then the Moor's. They drank cheerfully to each other's health, the Princess using all her art to win him with her words. The unsuspecting Moor supposed all this to be heartfelt and true; he did not know that this love of hers was but a snare to destroy him. When they had finished eating and the wine had vanquished his brain, the Princess said, 'We have a custom in our country; I do not know if you observe it here.'

'And what is this custom?' he asked.

'When dinner is over,' she replied, 'each one takes his companion's cup and drinks from it.'

She thereupon took his cup and filled it with wine for herself; then she ordered the maid to give him her cup, in which the wine had already been mixed with the drug. The girl acted her part well, for all the maids and servants in the palace wished his death and were in league with their mistress to destroy him. So the girl gave him the cup, while the drunken Moor, flattered by this show of love, imagined himself to be Alexander the Great in all his glory.

'Dearest,' the Princess said, swaying from side to side and placing her hand in his, 'here I have your cup and you have mine. Thus shall we drink from one another's cup.'

The Princess kissed his glass and drank; then she went over to him and kissed him on the cheek. The delighted Moor wanted to do the same; he raised the cup to his lips and gulped it down. At once he rolled over on his back like a dead man, and the cup fell from his hand. The Princess rejoiced, and the maids rushed out to the door of the palace to admit their master Aladdin.

Aladdin hastened to his wife's room and found her sitting at the table, with the Moor lying motionless before her. He took her joyfully into his arms and thanked her for all that she had done.

'Now go with your maids into the inner room,' he said, 'and leave me to myself awhile. I have some work to do.'

When they were all gone, Aladdin locked the door behind them and, going over to the magician, thrust his hand into the breast of his robe and took out the lamp. Then he drew his sword and cut off the Moor's head. Aladdin rubbed the lamp, and at once the jinnee appeared.

'I am here, master, I am here,' he said. 'What would you have?'

'I order you,' Aladdin said, 'to lift up this palace and set it down where it stood before, in front of the Sultan's palace in China.'

'I hear and obey, my master,' the jinnee replied.

Aladdin went in and sat down with his wife. Meanwhile, the jinnee carried the palace and set it down on its former site, in front of the Sultan's palace. Aladdin ordered the maids to bring the table, and he and the Princess feasted and made merry to their hearts' content. Next morning he got up and awakened his wife. The maids came in and dressed the Princess, and Aladdin dressed himself also. The two looked forward eagerly to meeting the Sultan.

★

As for the Sultan, after setting Aladdin free, he continued to grieve over the loss of his daughter; he passed his days wailing like a woman for her, his one and only child. Every morning, as he left his bed, he would look out toward the spot where Aladdin's palace had been, and weep until his eyes were dry and his eyelids sore. Rising that day as usual, he opened the window and looked out and saw before him a building. He rubbed his eyes and stared intently at it, until he had no doubt that it was Aladdin's palace. He at once called for his horse and rode over to his son-in-law's dwelling.

When Aladdin saw him approaching he went down and met him in the middle of the square. Taking him by the hand, he led him up to the Princess' room. Badr-al-Budur was overjoyed at her father's arrival. The Sultan caught his daughter in his arms, and the two mingled their joyful tears together. Then he asked her how she was and what had happened to her.

'Father,' she replied, 'my spirits did not revive until yesterday, when I saw my husband. He rescued me from a vile Moorish magician. Had it not been for Aladdin I would never have escaped from him, nor would you have seen me again in all your life. I had been pining with grief, not only because I was taken away from you, but also because I was separated from my husband. I shall ever be bound to him in gratitude for delivering me from that wicked enchanter.'

The Princess related to the Sultan all that happened.

'If you doubt our story, Your Majesty,' added Aladdin, 'come along and look at the magician's body.'

The Sultan followed Aladdin into the apartment and saw the corpse. He ordered his men to take it out and burn it and scatter the ashes to the winds.

'Forgive me, my son,' he said to Aladdin, 'for the injustice I have done you. I may well be excused for what I did, for I thought I had lost my only daughter, who is dearer to me than all my kingdom. You know the great love parents bear their children; mine is greater still, for I have none besides Badr-al-Budur.'

'Great Sultan,' Aladdin replied, 'you have done me no wrong, nor have I offended against Your Majesty. It was all the fault of that wicked magician.'

The Sultan ordered the city to be decorated. The streets were gaily decked, and a month of celebrations was observed in all the kingdom, to mark the return of Badr-al-Budur and her husband.

Nevertheless, Aladdin was not yet entirely safe from danger, although the magician's body had been burned and its ashes scattered to the winds. The detestable fellow had a brother viler than himself, and as skilled in magic and divination. As the proverb has it, they were as like as the two halves of a split pea. Each dwelt in a different corner of the earth and filled it with his witchcraft, guile, and malice.

Now, it chanced that one day this magician wished to know what had become of his brother. He therefore cast the sand, marked out the figures, and scanned them carefully. He learned to his dismay that his brother was dead. He cast the sand a second time, to see how he had died and where. He discovered that he had died a hideous death in a palace in China at the hands of a youth called Aladdin. Thereupon he rose and made ready for a journey. He traveled over deserts and plains and mountains for many months until he arrived in China and entered the capital where Aladdin lived. There he put up at the foreigners' inn and, after resting a little, went down to walk about the streets in search of some means to avenge his brother's death. Presently he came to a coffee shop in the market. It was a large place and many people were gathered there, some playing backgammon and others chess. He sat at one of the tables and heard those next to him talk of a saintly woman called Fatimah who practiced her devotions in a cell outside the town and came to the city only twice a month. She was renowned for her healing powers.

'Now I have found what I was looking for,' said the magician to himself. 'By means of this woman I will carry out my design.'

Then, turning to the people who were praising her virtues, he said to one of them, 'Good sir, who is this holy woman, and where does she live?'

'Why, man,' his neighbor cried, 'who has not heard of Mistress Fatimah's miracles? It is evident you are a stranger here, never to have heard of her piety, her long fasts, and her religious exercises.'

'You are right, sir, I am a stranger,' said the magician. 'I arrived in your city only last night. Pray tell me about the miracles of this good woman and where she lives. I have been down on my luck lately, and wish to go to her and seek her prayers, so that I may find comfort in them.'

The man told him of the miracles of Holy Fatimah and her saintliness. Then he took him by the hand and showed him the way to her dwelling in a cave at the top of a little mountain. The magician thanked the man for the trouble he had taken, and then returned to his lodgings.

As chance would have it, the following day Fatimah herself came down to the city. The magician left his lodgings in the morning and noticed the people crowding in the street. He went up to inquire the cause of the hubbub, and found the hermit standing in their midst. All the sick and ailing thronged about her, asking for her blessings and her prayers. As soon as she touched them they were cured. The magician followed her about until she returned to her cave, and then waited for nightfall. When evening came he entered a wine shop, drank a glass of liquor, and made his way to Holy Fatimah's cell. He found her fast asleep, lying on her back on a piece of matting. He stole toward her without a sound, sat on her stomach, and woke her up. She opened her eyes and was terrified to see a stranger crouching over her.

'Listen!' he cried. 'If you breathe one syllable or scream I will kill you. So get up and do as you are told.' And he swore to her that if she did his bidding he would not harm her. Then he rose and helped her to her feet.

'First,' he said, 'take my clothes and give me yours.' She gave him her clothes, together with her headdress, shawl, and veil.

'Now,' said the magician, 'you must stain me with some ointment to make my face the same color as yours.'

The old woman went to a corner and fetched a jar of ointment; she took some in the palm of her hand and rubbed his face with it until its color became like hers. She also gave him her staff and taught him how to walk with it, and what to do when he went down to the city. Finally she placed her beads around his neck and handed him a mirror.

'Look,' she said. 'There is not the slightest difference now between us.'

The magician looked into the mirror and saw that he was indeed her very image. Having gained his objective, he now broke his oath and slew the poor old woman. In the morning he made his way to the city and stood in front of Aladdin's palace. The people gathered around him, taking him for Holy Fatimah. He did all the things she used to do; he laid his hand on the sick and ailing and recited hymns and prayers for them. Hearing the noise, the Princess ordered one of the servants to find out what was going on. He went to look and presently returned.

'Mistress,' he said, 'it is Holy Fatimah, curing people by her touch. If it is your wish, I will call her in, so that you may receive her blessing.'

'Go and bring her to me,' said the Princess. 'I have heard tell of her miracles and virtues and would much like to see her.'

The servant brought in the magician, disguised in Fatimah's clothes. On coming to the Princess he offered up a long prayer for her continued health, and no one doubted that he was the saint herself. The Princess got up to receive him; she greeted him and made him sit down beside her. 'Mistress Fatimah,' she said, 'I wish you to stay with me always, so that I may obtain your blessing and follow your example in the ways of piety and goodness.'

This invitation was the very thing the magician wanted. But to complete his deception, he said, 'I am a poor woman, my lady. I pass my days in a solitary cave. Hermits like myself are not fitted to live in a palace.'

'Do not worry about that,' the Princess replied. 'I will give you a room of your own in my house, where you can worship undisturbed.'

'I am in duty bound to obey you, my lady,' said the magician. 'Only I beg you to let me eat and drink and sit in my room by myself, with no one to intrude on me.' He requested this for fear he should lift his veil while eating and expose his plot.

'Fear nothing, Mistress Fatimah,' said the Princess. 'It shall be as you wish. Get up now, and I will show you your room.' She led the disguised magician to the place she had assigned for the holy woman's use.

'Mistress Fatimah,' she said, 'this room is yours alone. Here you will live in peace and quiet.'

The magician thanked her for her kindness and called down blessings upon her. The Princess then showed him the jeweled dome with its four and twenty windows, and asked him what he thought of it.

'It is truly beautiful, my daughter,' the magician replied. 'There cannot be another place like it in the whole world. Yet I can see that it lacks one thing.'

'And what may that be, Mistress Fatimah?' asked the Princess.

'The egg of a bird called the roc,' said the magician. 'If that were hung from the middle of the dome, this hall would be the wonder of the world.'

'What is this bird,' asked the Princess, 'and where can its egg be found?'

'It is a huge bird, my lady,' the villain replied. 'Its strength and size are such that it can carry camels and elephants in its claws and fly with them. This bird is mostly found in the Mountain of Kaf. The builder who constructed this palace can bring you one of its eggs.'

It was now lunchtime. The slave girls laid the table, and the Princess invited her guest to eat with her. The magician, however, declined. He retired to his own room, where he ate by himself.

In the evening, Aladdin came home. Finding his wife thoughtful and anxious, he asked her the cause in some alarm.

'It is nothing at all, dearest,' she answered. 'I always thought there was nothing missing or deficient in our palace. Yet . . . if only a roc's egg were hung from the jeweled dome of the hall, our palace would be unrivaled in the world.'

'If that is all,' Aladdin replied, 'there is nothing simpler. Cheer up, my sweet. Just name the thing you fancy and I will bring it to you upon the instant, even if it be hidden in the darkest caverns of the earth.'

Leaving his wife, Aladdin went into his room, took out the lamp, and rubbed it; and at once the jinnee appeared before him, saying, 'Ask what you will!'

'I wish you to bring me a roc's egg,' said Aladdin, 'and to hang it in the dome of the palace.'

But the jinnee scowled on hearing these words.

'Ungrateful human,' he roared. 'Are you not content to have me and all the other slaves of the lamp at your beck and call? Must you also command me to bring you the sacred egg of our mistress and hang it in the dome of the palace for your amusement? By heaven, you and your wife deserve to be burned alive this instant. But as you are both ignorant of this offense and have no knowledge of its consequences, I forgive you. You are not to blame. The real offender is that wicked magician, the Moor's brother, who is now staying in your palace disguised as Holy Fatimah. He put on her clothes and killed her in her cave, then he came here to avenge his brother's death. It was he who prompted your wife to make this request.'

And so saying, the jinnee vanished.

Aladdin was thunderstruck when he heard this, and all his limbs trembled with fear. But he soon recovered himself, thought of a plan, and went back to his wife, saying that his head ached; for he knew that the holy woman was renowned for her healing powers. The Princess sent at once for Fatimah, so that she might lay her hand on his head.

'Fatimah will soon cure you of your pain,' she said, and told him that she had invited the saintly woman to stay with her in the palace.

Presently the magician came in; Aladdin rose to receive him and, pretending to know nothing of his intent, welcomed him as he might have welcomed the holy woman herself.

'Mistress Fatimah,' he said, 'I beg you to do me a kindness. I have long heard of your great skill in curing ailments. Now I have a violent pain in my head.'

The magician could scarcely believe his ears, for he wished for nothing better. He came near and, laying one hand on Aladdin's head, stretched the other under his robe and drew out his dagger to kill him. But Aladdin was on his guard; he caught him by the wrist, wrenched the weapon from him, and thrust it into his heart.

'Oh, what a woeful crime!' exclaimed the terrified Princess. 'Have you no fear of heaven to kill Fatimah, this virtuous and saintly woman, whose miracles are the wonder of our time?'

'Know then,' Aladdin replied, 'that the villain whom I have killed was not Fatimah but the man who murdered her. This is the brother of the Moorish magician who carried you off by his magic to Africa. He came to this country and thought of this trick. He murdered the old woman, disguised himself in her habit, and came here to avenge his brother's death on me. It was he who incited you to ask for a roc's egg, for that was a sure way to destroy me. If you doubt my words, come and see who it is that I have slain.'

Aladdin lifted off the magician's veil, and the Princess saw a man in disguise. At once the truth dawned upon her.

'My love,' she said, 'this is the second time I have put you in danger of your life.'

'Never mind, Badr-al-Budur,' Aladdin replied, 'I gladly accept whatever befalls me through you.'

He took her into his arms and kissed her, and they loved each other more than ever.

At that moment the Sultan arrived. They told him all that had happened and showed him the magician's body. The Sultan ordered that the corpse be burned and the ashes scattered to the winds, like his brother's.

Aladdin dwelt with the Princess in contentment and joy, and thereafter escaped all dangers. When the Sultan died, Aladdin inherited his throne and reigned justly over the kingdom. All his subjects loved him, and he lived happily with Badr-al-Budur until death overtook them.

The Donkey

Two rogues once saw a simple-looking fellow leading a donkey on the end of a long rope on a deserted road.

'Watch this,' said one to the other. 'I will take that beast and make a fool of its master. Come along and you will see.'

He crept up behind the simple fellow without a sound, unfastened the rope from the donkey, and put it around his own neck. He then jogged along in the donkey's place, while his friend made off with the beast.

Suddenly the thief, with the donkey's rope

around his neck, stopped in his tracks and would go no farther. The silly fellow, feeling the pull on the rope, looked over his shoulder, and was utterly amazed to find his donkey changed into a human being.

'Who in heaven's name are you?' he cried.

'Sir,' the thief replied, 'I am your donkey; but my story is quite extraordinary. It all happened one day when I came home very drunk – as I always did. My poor old mother scolded me terribly and begged me to mend my ways. But I took my stick and beat her. In her anger she called down Allah's curse upon me, and I was at once changed into the donkey that has served you faithfully all these years. My mother must have taken pity on me and prayed today to the Almighty to change me back into human shape.'

'Good Heavens!' cried the simpleton, who believed every word of the rascal's story. 'Please forgive all that I have done to you and all the hardships you put up with in my service.'

He let the robber go and returned home, bewildered and upset.

'What has come over you, and where is your donkey?' asked his wife when she saw him.

He told her the strange story.

'Allah will be angry with us,' the woman cried, wringing her hands, 'for having used a human being so cruelly.'

And she fell down on her knees, praying for forgiveness.

For several days afterward the simple fellow stayed idle at home. At last his wife told him to go and buy another donkey, so that he could do some useful work again. He went off to the market, and as he was taking a look at the animals on sale, he was astonished to see his own donkey among them. When he had identified the beast beyond all doubt, he whispered in its ear, 'Well, you old scoundrel! Have you been drinking and beating your mother again? Upon my life, I will not buy you *this* time!'

The Tale of Khalifah the Fisherman

Once upon a time, in the reign of the Caliph Harun al-Rashid, there lived in the city of Baghdad a poor fisherman called Khalifah.

It so happened one morning that he took his net upon his back and went down to the river Tigris before the other fishermen arrived. When he reached the bank he rolled up his sleeves and tucked his robe into his belt; then he spread his net and cast it into the water. He cast his net ten times, but did not catch a single fish. In despair, he waded knee-deep into the river and threw his net as far as he could. He waited patiently for a long time, and then pulled hard on the cords. When at last he managed to haul the heavy net ashore, he was astonished to find in it a lame, one-eyed monkey. His astonishment quickly changed to frustration and anger. Tying the beast to a tree, he was on the point of lashing it with his whip when the monkey spoke in the voice of a human.

'Stay your hand, Khalifah,' it pleaded. 'Do not whip me. Cast your net again and you will soon have what you desire.'

The fisherman once more spread his net and cast it into the water. After some time he felt the net grow heavy, but on bringing it to land, he was vexed to find in it another monkey, even more strange-looking than the first. Its eyelids were black and long, its hands were dyed with red, and it wore a tattered vest about the middle. Its front teeth, set wide apart, gleamed as it stared at the fisherman with an awkward grin.

'Praise be to Allah, who has changed the fishes of the river into monkeys!' exclaimed Khalifah. Then, running toward the first animal, he cried, 'So this is the result of your advice! I began my day with the sight of your monstrous face and I shall doubtless end it in starvation and ruin.'

He brandished his whip high above his head and was about to fall again upon the one-eyed monkey when it begged him for mercy.

'Spare me, Khalifah, in the name of Allah!' it cried. 'Go to my brother. He will give you good advice.'

The bewildered fisherman flung away his whip and turned to the second monkey.

'If you mark my words and do as I tell you, Khalifah,' said the second monkey, 'you shall prosper.'

'Well, what do you want me to do?' the fisherman asked.

'Leave me on this bank,' came the reply, 'and once more cast your net.'

The fisherman spread his net again and cast it into the water. He waited patiently, and when he felt the net grow heavy, he gently drew it in, only to land yet another monkey, which had red hair and wore a blue vest about its middle.

'Surely this is a cursed day from first to last!' exclaimed the fisherman when he saw the third monkey. 'There is surely not a single fish left in the river and we shall have nothing today but monkeys!'

Then, turning to the red-haired beast, he cried, 'In heaven's name, what are you?'

'Do you not know who I am, Khalifah?' the monkey replied.

'Indeed I do not!' protested the fisherman.

'Know, then, that I am the monkey of Abu Ahmad, chief of the money-changers. To me he owes his good fortune and all his wealth. When I bless him in the morning he gains five pieces of gold, and when I say good night to him he gains five more.'

'Mark that,' the fisherman said, turning to the

first beast. '*You* cannot boast of such blessings. Seeing your face this morning has brought me nothing but bad luck!'

'Leave my brother in peace, Khalifah,' said the red-haired monkey, 'and cast your net once more into the river. After that, come back and show me your catch. I will teach you how to use it to your best advantage.'

'I hear and obey, King of all monkeys!' the fisherman answered.

Khalifah did as the monkey told him, and when he drew in his net he rejoiced to find a splendid fish with a large head, broad fins, and eyes that glittered like gold coins. Marveling at the quaintness of his prize, he took it and showed it to the red-haired animal.

'Now gather some fresh grass,' said the monkey, 'and spread it at the bottom of your basket; lay the fish upon it and cover it with more grass. Then carry the basket to Baghdad. Should anyone speak to you on your way, you must not answer, but go directly to the market of the money-changers. In the middle of it stands the shop of Abu Ahmad, their chief. You will find him sitting on a mattress with an embroidered cushion at his back, surrounded by his slaves and servants. In front of him you will see two boxes, one for gold and one for silver. Go up to him, set your basket before him, and say, "Sir, I went down to the river Tigris this morning and in your name cast my net. I caught this fish." He will ask, "Have you shown it to any other man?" "No," you must answer.

'Then he will take the fish and offer you one piece of gold. You must refuse to sell it for that price. He will offer you two gold pieces, but you must still refuse. Whatever he offers, you must not accept, though it be the fish's weight in gold. He will ask, "What, then, do you want?" And you will reply, "I will exchange this fish for nothing more than a few simple words." "What are they?" he will ask, and you will answer, "Stand up and say, *Bear witness, all who are present in this market, that I give Khalifah the fisherman my monkey in exchange for his monkey, and that I barter my fortune for his fortune*. That is the price of my fish: I demand no gold."

'If he agrees to this,' went on the red-haired beast, 'you will become my master; I will bless you every morning and every evening, and you will gain ten pieces of gold every day. As for Abu Ahmad, he will be plagued with the sight of my lame, one-eyed brother, and will suffer heavy losses. Bear in mind what I have told you, Khalifah, and you will prosper.'

'I will obey you in every particular, royal monkey!' the fisherman replied. He untied the three animals, who leaped into the water and disappeared.

Khalifah washed the fish, placed it in his basket upon some fresh grass, and covered it over. Then he set out for the city, singing merrily.

As he made his way through the streets, many people greeted him and asked if he had any fish to sell. But he walked on without a word until he reached the market of the money-changers and stopped before Abu Ahmad's shop. The fisherman saw Abu Ahmad surrounded by numerous servants who waited upon him with such ceremony as can be found only in the courts of kings. He went up to the money-changer.

'Fisherman, what can we do for you?' Abu Ahmad asked.

'Chief of the money-changers,' Khalifah replied, 'this morning I went down to the Tigris, and in your name cast my net. I caught this fish.'

'What a strange coincidence!' cried the delighted money-changer. 'A holy man appeared to me in a dream last night, saying, "You will receive a present from me tomorrow." This must surely be the present. Only tell me, on your life, have you shown this fish to any other man?'

'No,' the fisherman replied. 'No one else has seen it.'

The money-changer turned to one of his slaves and said, 'Take this fish to my house and ask my daughter to have it dressed for dinner. Tell her to fry one half and to grill the other.'

'I hear and obey,' answered the slave, and departed with the fish to his master's house.

Abu Ahmad took a piece of gold from one of his coffers and offered it to the fisherman.

'Spend this on your family,' he said.

Now, Khalifah, who had never before earned such money for a single day's labor, instinctively held out his hand and took the coin. But as he was about to leave the shop, he remembered the monkey's instructions.

'Take this and give me back my fish,' he cried, throwing down the coin. 'Would you make a fool of me?'

Thinking that the fisherman was jesting, Abu Ahmad smiled, then handed him three gold pieces; but Khalifah refused the gold.

'Since when have you known me to sell my fish for such a trifle?' he asked.

Abu Ahmad then gave him five pieces. 'Take these,' he said, 'and do not be greedy.'

The fisherman took the gold and left the shop, scarcely believing his eyes. 'Glory be to God!' he thought. 'The Caliph himself has not so much gold in his coffers as I have in my purse today!'

It was not until he reached the end of the market place that he recalled the monkey's advice. He hurried back to the money-changer and again threw down the coins before him.

'What has come over you, Khalifah?' asked Abu Ahmad. 'Would you rather have the money in silver?'

'I want neither your gold nor your silver,' the fisherman retorted. 'Give me back my fish.'

'I have given you five pieces of gold for a fish that is hardly worth ten coppers,' exclaimed the money-changer angrily, 'and yet you are not satisfied.' Then, turning to his slaves, he cried, 'Take hold of this rascal and thrash him soundly!'

The slaves immediately set upon the fisherman and beat him until their master called, 'Enough!' But as soon as they let go of him, Khalifah rose to his feet as though he had felt no pain at all. 'Sir,' he said, 'you should have known that I can take more blows than ten donkeys put together.'

At this Abu Ahmad laughed.

'Enough of this fooling,' he said. 'How much do you want?'

'Only a few simple words,' the fisherman replied. 'I just want you to get up and say: "Bear witness, all who are present in this market, that I give Khalifah the fisherman my monkey in exchange for his monkey, and that I barter my fortune for his fortune."'

'Nothing could be easier than that,' Abu Ahmad said and, rising to his feet, made the declaration. Then, turning to the fisherman, he asked, 'Is that all?'

'It is.'

'Then I bid you good day.'

Khalifah put the empty basket on his shoulder and hurried back to the river. As soon as he reached the bank he spread his net and cast it into the water. When he drew it in, he found it filled with fish of every kind. Presently a woman came up to him with a basket and bought a gold piece's worth of fish. Then a slave passed by and also bought a gold piece's worth. When the day was done, Khalifah had earned ten pieces of gold. And he continued to earn this sum day after day until he had a hundred pieces of gold.

Now, the fisherman lived in a hovel of a house at the end of the Lane of the Merchants. One night, as he lay in his lodging overcome with drink, he said to himself, 'All your neighbors, Khalifah, think you are a penniless old fisherman. They have not seen your hundred pieces of gold. But they will soon hear of your wealth; and before long the Caliph himself will get to know of it. One day, when his treasury is empty, he will send for you and say, "I need some money. I hear you have a hundred gold pieces. You must lend them to me." "Sire," I will answer, "your slave is a poor, humble fisherman. The man who told you that is a wicked liar." The Caliph, of course, will not believe me. He will hand me over to the governor, who will strip me naked and whip me mercilessly. My best course, therefore, is to get my body used to the whip. I will get up now and prepare myself.'

Khalifah took off all his clothes. He placed beside him an old leather cushion, took up his whip, and began lashing himself, aiming every other stroke at the cushion and yelling out, 'A wicked lie! Oh, oh! I have no money!'

His cries and the sound of the whipping echoed in the stillness of the night and startled the neighbors out of their beds. They rushed out into the street, inquiring the cause of the disturbance.

Thinking that thieves had broken into the fisherman's house, they hurried to his rescue. To their surprise, the door was locked and bolted.

'The thieves must have got in from the terrace next door,' they said to each other. So they climbed up to the adjoining terrace and from there descended into the house. They found the naked fisherman whipping himself.

'What the devil has possessed you tonight, Khalifah?' his neighbors cried in amazement. And when he had told them the very secret he had been anxious to keep from them, they laughed at him and said, 'Enough of this joke, you stupid man! May you have no joy in your treasure!'

When the fisherman woke up the next morning he was still worried about his gold. 'If I leave my money at home,' he said to himself, 'I know it will be stolen. If I carry it in my belt, thieves will waylay me in some deserted place and cut my throat, and rob me of it. I must think of a better device.'

Finally he decided to sew a pocket inside the breast of his robe, and to carry the gold there tied in a bundle. This done, he took up his net, his basket, and his stick and went down to the Tigris.

On reaching the river he stepped down the bank and cast his net into the water. But the net brought up nothing at all. Farther and farther he moved along the bank until he had traveled half a day's journey from the capital; but all to no purpose. At last he summoned up all his strength and hurled the net with such desperate force that the bundle of coins flew out of his pocket and plunged into the river.

Khalifah cast off his clothes and dived after the gold; but it was swept away by the current, and soon he had to abandon the search. Covered with mud and utterly exhausted, he walked back to the spot where he had left his clothes. But they were nowhere to be found.

In despair, he wrapped himself in his net and, like a raging camel, ran wildly up and down the bank.

So much for Khalifah the fisherman.

Now, it so chanced that the Caliph Harun al-Rashid (who is the other important figure in our tale) had at that time a friend among the jewelers of Baghdad called Sheikh Kirnas. He was known to all the merchants of the city as the Caliph's own broker; and his influence was such that nothing choice or rare, from jewels to slave girls, was put up for sale without being first shown to him.

One day, as Sheikh Kirnas was attending to his customers, the chief of the brokers brought into his shop a slave girl of astonishing beauty. Not only had she no equal in good looks, but she was also graced with many accomplishments. She could recite pretty verses, sing, and make music on all manner of instruments. Her name was Kut-al-Kulub. Sheikh Kirnas bought her right away for five thousand pieces of gold, and after he had dressed her in rich robes and adorned her with jewels worth a thousand more, he took her to his master the Caliph.

Al-Rashid was so delighted with her talents that next morning he sent for Sheikh Kirnas and gave him ten thousand pieces in payment for the girl. The Caliph loved his new favorite so deeply that for her sake he forsook his wife, the Lady Zubaidah, and all his other concubines. He stayed by her side for a whole month, leaving her only when he attended the public prayers.

It was not long, however, before the courtiers and officers of state became dissatisfied with their master's conduct. Unable to keep silent any longer, they complained to Jaafar, the Grand Vizier.

One day, while attending the Caliph at the mosque, Jaafar discreetly hinted at his master's excessive attachment to the slave girl.

'By Allah, Jaafar,' the Caliph replied, 'my will is powerless in this matter, for my heart is caught in the snare of love, and try as I may, I cannot release it.'

'Commander of the Faithful,' said the vizier, 'this girl is now a member of your household, a servant among your servants. Think of the pleasures of riding and hunting and other sports, for these may help you to forget her.'

'You have spoken wisely, Jaafar,' the Caliph replied. 'Come, we will go hunting this very day.'

As soon as the prayers were over, they mounted

their steeds and rode out to the open country followed by the troops.

It was a hot day. When they had traveled a long way from the city, Al-Rashid, feeling thirsty, looked around to see if there was a sign of any encampment nearby. He observed an object far off on a mound. 'Can you see what that is?' he asked Jaafar.

'It looks like a man,' the vizier replied. 'He is perhaps the keeper of an orchard or a cucumber garden. Maybe he can give us some water to drink. I will ride and fetch some.'

But Al-Rashid ordered Jaafar to wait for the troops, who had lingered behind, and he himself galloped off more swiftly than the desert wind or the waterfall that thunders down the rocks. On reaching the hillside he found a man swathed in a fishing net, with hair disheveled and dusty, and bloodshot eyes blazing like torches.

Al-Rashid politely greeted the strange-looking figure, and Khalifah (for the man was no other than our fisherman) muttered a few angry words in reply.

'Have you a drink of water to give me?' the Caliph asked.

'Are you blind or stupid?' broke out the fisherman. 'Can you not see that the river Tigris flows behind this hillock?'

Al-Rashid walked around the hillock and found that the river did indeed run behind it; so he drank and watered his horse. Then he returned to Khalifah.

'What are you doing here?' he asked. 'What is your trade?'

'This question is even sillier than the last!' cried Khalifah. 'Do you not see my net about my shoulders?'

'So you are a fisherman,' said the Caliph. 'But where have you left your cloak, your gown, and your belt?'

Now these were the very things that had been stolen from the fisherman. Therefore, when he heard them named, he did not doubt that the thief stood before him. At once he darted forward, swift as a flash of lightning, and caught the Caliph's horse by the bridle.

'Give me back my clothes,' he shouted, 'and stop this foolish joke!'

'By Allah, my friend,' the Caliph replied, 'I have never seen your clothes, nor can I understand what you are shouting about.'

Now, Al-Rashid had a small mouth and round, plump cheeks, so that Khalifah took him for a piper or a flute player.

'Give me back my clothes, you scraper of beggarly tunes,' he threatened, 'or I will cudgel your bones with this stick.'

When he saw the fisherman brandishing his heavy stick, the Caliph thought to himself, 'By Allah, one stroke from this cudgel will be the end of me.'

So, to humor Khalifah, he took off his splendid satin cloak and handed it to him.

'Here,' he said, 'take this in place of the things you lost.'

'My clothes were worth ten times as much,' muttered the fisherman as he turned the cloak about with obvious contempt.

Al-Rashid prevailed upon him to try it on. Finding it too long, Khalifah took the knife that was attached to the handle of his basket and cut off the lower part of the cloak, so that it hung just above his knees.

'Tell me, good piper,' he said, 'how much money does your playing bring you in a month?'

'Ten pieces of silver,' the Caliph replied.

'By Allah, you make me feel sorry for you,' the fisherman said. 'Why, I make ten gold pieces a day. If you are willing to enter my service, I will teach you my trade and make you my partner. In this way you will earn a good round sum every day. And if your present master does not like it, this stick of mine will protect you.'

'I accept your offer,' the Caliph replied.

'Then get off your horse and follow me,' the fisherman said. 'We will begin work this instant.'

Al-Rashid dismounted and tethered his horse to a nearby tree. Then he rolled up his sleeves and tucked his robe into his belt.

'Hold the net thus,' said the fisherman; 'spread it over your arm thus, and cast it into the water – thus.'

Al-Rashid summoned up all his strength and did as the fisherman told him. When, after a few moments, he tried to draw the net in, it was so heavy that the fisherman had to come to his aid.

'Dog!' shouted Khalifah, as the two tugged together at the cords, 'if you tear or damage my net I will take your horse from you and beat you black and blue. Do you hear?'

When at last they managed to haul the net ashore, they saw that it was filled with fish of every kind and color.

'Useless old piper though you are,' said Khalifah, 'you may yet become an excellent fisherman. Off with you now to the market, and fetch me two large baskets. I will stay here and watch over the fish till you return. Then we will load the catch on your horse's back and take it to the fish market. Your job will be to hold the scales and receive the money. Go, waste no time!'

'I hear and obey,' replied the Caliph and, mounting his horse, galloped away, scarcely able to contain his laughter.

When Al-Rashid rejoined Jaafar and the troops, the vizier, who had been anxiously waiting for him, said, 'You no doubt came upon some pleasant garden on the way where you rested all this time.'

At this the Caliph burst out laughing, and he proceeded to tell the company of his adventure with the fisherman. 'My master is now waiting for me,' he went on. 'We are going to the market, to sell the fish and share the profit.'

'Then let me provide you with some customers,'

said the vizier, laughing. But a mischievous fancy took hold of the Caliph's mind.

'By the honor of my ancestors,' he cried, 'whoever brings me a fish from my master Khalifah shall receive one gold piece from me.'

And so a crier proclaimed the Caliph's wish among the guards and they all made for the river, in the direction of the hillock. The fisherman, still waiting for Al-Rashid (and the baskets), was astounded to see the guards swoop upon him like vultures, each grabbing as many fish as his hands could hold.

'There must surely be something very odd about these fish!' thought the terrified Khalifah. 'O Allah, send the piper quickly to my aid!' And to protect himself from the raiders, he jumped right into the water with a fish in each hand.

The guards wrapped up the spoil in their large, gold-embroidered handkerchiefs and rode back to their master at full gallop. As soon as they were gone, however, the Caliph's chief footman arrived.

'Come here, fisherman,' he said, when he saw Khalifah holding up the fish.

'Away with you, villain!' Khalifah shouted.

But the footman came nearer. 'Give me your fish,' he said persuasively. 'I will pay you for them.'

The fisherman still refused, and the footman lifted his lance and aimed it at him.

'Dog, do not throw!' Khalifah cried. 'I would rather give you all than lose my life.'

So saying, he scornfully threw the fish at the

footman, who picked them up and wrapped them in his handkerchief. Then the footman thrust his hand into his pocket in order to pay the fisherman. But, as chance would have it, there was no money there.

'I am afraid you have no luck today,' he said, 'for I have not a copper about me. If you will come to the Caliph's palace tomorrow and ask for Sandal, the chief footman, you will receive a hearty welcome and a generous reward.'

With this the footman leaped upon his horse and galloped away.

'This is indeed a joyless day!' groaned the fisherman. In despair he threw his net upon his shoulder and set out for the market.

As he walked through the streets of Baghdad, passers-by were puzzled to see a fisherman wearing a valuable satin cloak. Presently he entered the market place and passed by the shop of the Caliph's own tailor. The tailor recognized the garment, for he had made it himself. He called out to Khalifah.

'Where did you get that cloak?' he asked.

'What is it to you?' returned the fisherman angrily. 'Yet, if you must know, it was given me by an apprentice of mine. The rascal had stolen my clothes; I took pity on him and, rather than have his hand cut off for theft, I accepted this thing in exchange.'

The tailor was much amused to hear this and realized that the fisherman was the victim of the Caliph's latest prank.

Meanwhile, at the palace a plot was being

hatched against the Caliph's favorite, Kut-al-Kulub. For when the Lady Zubaidah, his Queen, learned of her husband's new attachment, she became so jealous that she refused to eat or drink, and busily schemed to avenge herself on the slave girl. Hearing that Al-Rashid had gone hunting, she held a feast in her room and sent for Kut-al-Kulub to entertain the guests with her singing. The unsuspecting girl took up her instruments and was conducted to the Queen's chamber.

When her eyes fell on Kut-al-Kulub, the Lady Zubaidah could not help admiring the girl's exquisite beauty. She concealed her scheming thoughts and with a welcoming smile ordered her to sit down. The girl sang to the accompaniment of the lute and the tambourine. So sweetly did she sing that her audience was charmed into a magic trance, the birds paused in their flight, and the entire palace seemed to echo with a thousand voices.

'Al-Rashid is hardly to blame for loving her,' thought the Lady Zubaidah, as the girl ended her song and gracefully bowed to the ground before her.

The servants set before Kut-al-Kulub a dish of sweetmeats into which the Queen had mixed a powerful drug. Scarcely had the girl swallowed a mouthful than her head fell backward and she sank to the ground unconscious. The Lady Zubaidah ordered her maids to carry the girl to her private room. Then, by her order, an announcement was made that Kut-al-Kulub had met with an accident and died. She also ordered a mock burial to take place in the grounds of the palace. The Queen threatened her servants with instant death if they revealed the secret.

When the Caliph returned from the hunt and news of his favorite's death was broken to him, the world darkened before his eyes and he was stricken with grief. He wept bitterly for Kut-al-Kulub and stayed by her supposed tomb for a long time.

Her plot having succeeded, the Lady Zubaidah ordered a trusted slave to lock the unconscious girl into a chest and carry it to the market. He was told to sell the chest immediately without revealing its contents.

Now to return to the fisherman. Early the next morning, Khalifah said to himself, 'I can do nothing better today than go to the Caliph's palace and ask his footman for the money he owes me.'

So off he went to Al-Rashid's court. As soon as he entered he saw Sandal, the Caliph's footman, in the doorway with a crowd of slaves waiting upon him. On the fisherman's approach, one of the slaves rose to bar his way and would have turned him back had not the footman recognized Khalifah. He greeted him with a laugh and, remembering the debt, put his hand into his pocket to take out his purse. At that moment, however, a shout was heard announcing the approach of Jaafar, the vizier. Sandal sprang to his feet, hurried off to the vizier, and fell into a long conversation with him.

Khalifah tried again and again to draw the

footman's attention to him, but all to no avail. At last the vizier took notice of him and asked, 'Who is that odd fellow?'

'That,' Sandal replied, 'is the selfsame fisherman whose fish we seized yesterday on the Caliph's orders.' And he went on to explain the reason for Khalifah's visit.

When he had heard Sandal's account, the vizier smiled. 'This fisherman,' he said, 'is the Caliph's instructor and business partner. He has indeed come at a time when we need him most. Today our master's heart is heavy with grief over the death of his loved one, and perhaps nothing will amuse him more than this fisherman's quaint humor. I will announce him to the Caliph.'

Jaafar hurried to the Caliph's room. He found him bowed down with sorrow over the loss of Kut-al-Kulub. The vizier wished him peace and, bowing low before him, said, 'On my way to you just now, Commander of the Faithful, I met at the door your teacher and partner, Khalifah, the fisherman. He is full of complaints against you. "Glory to Allah," I heard him say. "Is this how masters should be treated? I sent him to fetch a couple of baskets and he never came back."

'Now I pray you, Commander of the Faithful,' Jaafar went on, 'if you still have a mind to be his partner, let him know it; but if you wish to end your joint labors, tell him that he must seek another man.'

The Caliph smiled at Jaafar's words, and his sorrow seemed to be lightened.

'Is this true, Jaafar?' he asked. 'Upon my soul, this fisherman must be rewarded.'

Then he added, with a mischievous twinkle in his eye, 'If it is Allah's will that this man should prosper through me, it shall be done; and if it is his will that he should be punished through me, it shall be done also.'

So saying, Al-Rashid took out a large sheet of paper and cut it into numerous pieces.

'Write down on twenty of these papers,' he said to the vizier, 'sums of money from one piece of gold to a thousand; and on twenty more all the offices of state from the smallest clerkship to the Caliphate itself. Also twenty kinds of punishment from the lightest beating to a terrible death.'

'I hear and obey,' Jaafar replied, and he did as his master told him.

'I swear by my holy ancestors,' said Al-Rashid, 'that Khalifah the fisherman shall have the choice of one of these papers, and that I will accordingly reward him. Go and bring him before me.'

'There is no strength or help except in Allah,' said Jaafar to himself as he left the Caliph's room. 'Who knows what lies in store for this poor fellow?'

When he found the fisherman he took him by the hand and, followed by a crowd of slaves, conducted him through seven long corridors until they stood at the door of the Caliph's room.

'Be careful,' said the vizier to the terrified fisherman. 'You are about to be admitted to the presence of the Commander of the Faithful, Defender of the Faith.'

With this he led him in; and Khalifah, who was so overawed by the magnificence of his surroundings that he could not understand the vizier's words, suddenly saw the Caliph seated on a couch with all the officers of his court standing around him. The fisherman recognized his former apprentice.

'It is good to see you again, my piper!' he cried. 'But was it right to go away and leave me by the river all alone with the fish, and never return? Know, then, that thanks to your absence I was attacked by a band of mounted rogues, who carried off the entire catch. Had you returned promptly with the baskets we would have made a handsome profit. And what is worse, the ruffians have now put me under arrest. But tell me, who has imprisoned *you* in this dungeon?'

Al-Rashid smiled and held out the slips to the fisherman.

'Come closer, Khalifah,' he said, 'and draw me one of these papers.'

'Only yesterday you were a fisherman,' Khalifah remarked. 'Now I see that you have turned fortune-teller. Have you not heard the proverb "A rolling stone gathers no moss"?'

'Enough of this chatter,' said Jaafar sternly. 'Come, do as you are told: draw one of these papers.'

The fisherman picked out one paper and handed it to the Caliph.

'Good piper,' he said, 'read me my fortune and keep nothing from me.'

Al-Rashid passed the paper to his vizier and ordered him to read it aloud. Such was Khalifah's luck, however, that his choice was a hundred blows of the stick. Accordingly he was thrown down on the floor and given a hundred strokes.

'Commander of the Faithful,' Jaafar said, 'this unfortunate man has come to drink from the river of your charity and goodness. Do not send him away thirsty.'

The vizier persuaded the Caliph to let the fisherman draw once more. The second paper decreed that Khalifah should be given nothing at all. Jaafar, however, prevailed upon the Caliph to let the fisherman draw a third. Khalifah drew again, and the vizier unfolded the paper and announced, 'One gold piece.'

'What!' cried the angry fisherman. 'One piece for a hundred strokes? May Allah justly repay you for your wickedness!'

The Caliph laughed, and Jaafar took the fisherman by the hand and led him away from his master's presence. As Khalifah was leaving the palace, Sandal called out to him.

'Come, my friend,' he said, 'give me my share of the Caliph's reward.'

'You want your share, rascal, do you?' broke out the fisherman. 'All I earned was a hundred strokes and one piece of gold. You would indeed be welcome to one half of my beating;

as for the miserable coin, why, you can have that, too!'

He flung the coin at him and rushed off angrily. Moved with pity, Sandal ordered some slaves to run after him and bring him back. Sandal took out a red purse and emptied a hundred gold coins into Khalifah's hands.

'Here,' he said, 'take this in payment of my debt, and go home in peace.'

Khalifah rejoiced. He put the gold into his pocket, together with the coin that Al-Rashid had given him, and went out of the palace.

Now, it so happened that as he was walking home, lost in happy fancies, he came across a large crowd in the market place. Pushing his way among the merchants, he found that the center of attention was a large chest on which a young slave was sitting. Beside the chest stood an old man, who was calling out, 'Gentlemen, merchants, worthy citizens! Who will bid first for this chest of unknown treasure from the harem of the Lady Zubaidah, wife of the Commander of the Faithful?'

'By Allah,' said one of the merchants, 'I will bid twenty pieces of gold.'

'Fifty,' another cried.

'A hundred,' shouted a third.

'Who will give more?' inquired the auctioneer.

Breathless with excitement, Khalifah the fisherman shouted, 'Let it be mine for a hundred and one pieces!'

'The chest is yours,' the auctioneer replied. 'Hand

in your gold, and may Allah bless the bargain!'

Khalifah paid the slave, lifted the heavy chest with difficulty onto his shoulders, and carried it home. As he staggered along, he wondered what the precious contents might be. Presently he reached his dwelling, and after he had managed to get the chest through the door, he set to work to open it. But the chest was securely locked.

'What the devil possessed me to buy a box that cannot even be opened!' he cried.

Then he decided to break the chest to pieces, but it stoutly resisted all his blows and kicks. Utterly exhausted by the effort, he stretched himself out on the chest and fell asleep.

About an hour later he was awakened by a sound of movement underneath him. Out of his mind with terror, he leaped to his feet, crying, 'This chest must be haunted by demons! Praise be to Allah, who prevented me from opening it! Had I freed them in the dark they would surely have put me to a miserable death!'

His terror increased as the noise became more distinct. He searched in vain for a lamp, and finally rushed out into the street yelling at the top of his voice, 'Help! Help, good neighbors!'

Roused from their sleep, his neighbors peered from their doors and windows.

'What has happened?' they shouted.

'Devils!' the fisherman cried. 'My house is haunted by devils! Give me a lamp and a hammer, in the name of Allah!'

The neighbors laughed. One gave him a lamp and another a hammer. His confidence restored, he returned home determined to break open the chest. In the light of the lamp he battered the locks with the hammer and lifted the lid. What was this? – a girl as lovely as the moon. Her eyes were half open, as if she had just wakened from a heavy sleep. Khalifah marveled at her beauty.

'In Allah's name, who are you?' he whispered, kneeling down before her.

When she heard his words the girl regained her senses.

'Who are *you?* Where am I?' she asked, looking intently into his face.

'I am Khalifah, the fisherman, and you are in my house.' he answered.

'Am I not in the palace of the Caliph Harun al-Rashid?' asked the girl.

'Are you out of your mind?' the fisherman exclaimed. 'Let me tell you at once that you belong to no one but me; it was only this morning that I bought you for a hundred and one pieces of gold. Allah be praised for this lucky bargain!'

The girl was hungry. 'Give me something to eat,' she said.

'Alas,' the fisherman replied. 'There is nothing to eat or drink in this house. I myself have hardly tasted anything these two days.'

'Have you any money?' she asked.

'God preserve this chest!' he answered bitterly. 'This bargain has taken every coin I had.'

'Then go to your neighbors,' she said, 'and bring me something to eat, for I am famished.'

The fisherman rushed into the street again. 'Good neighbors,' he cried, 'who will give a hungry man something to eat?'

This he repeated several times at the top of his voice, until the unfortunate neighbors, awakened once more by his cries, opened their windows and threw down food to him; one gave him half a loaf of bread, another a piece of cheese, a third a cucumber. Returning home, he set the food before Kut-al-Kulub and invited her to eat.

'Bring me a drink of water,' she now said. 'I am very thirsty.'

So Khalifah took his empty pitcher and ran again into the street, begging the neighbors for some water. They replied with angry curses; but unable to stand his cries any longer, they carried water to him in buckets, jugs, and ewers. He filled his pitcher and took it to the slave girl.

When she had eaten and drunk, the fisherman asked her how she came to be locked inside the chest. She told him all that had happened at the Caliph's palace. 'This will make your fortune,' she added, 'for when Al-Rashid hears of my rescue, I know he will reward you.'

'But is not this Al-Rashid the foolish piper whom I taught how to fish?' Khalifah cried. 'Never in all my life have I met such a miserly rascal!'

'My friend,' said the girl, 'you must stop this senseless talk and make yourself worthy of the new station that awaits you. Above all, you must bear yourself respectfully and courteously in the presence of the Commander of the Faithful.'

Such was the influence of Kut-al-Kulub's words on Khalifah that a new world seemed to unfold before him. The dark veil of ignorance was lifted from his eyes and he became a wiser man.

Early the next morning Kut-al-Kulub asked Khalifah to bring her pen, ink, and paper. She wrote to Sheikh Kirnas, the Caliph's jeweler, telling him where she was and all that had happened. Then she sent the fisherman off with the letter.

Straight to the jeweler's he went and, on entering, bowed to the ground before the merchant and wished him peace. But, taking Khalifah for a beggar, the merchant ordered a slave to give him a copper and show him out. Khalifah refused the coin, saying, 'I beg no charity. Read this, I pray you.'

As soon as he finished reading the girl's letter, Sheikh Kirnas raised it to his lips; then he got up and gave the fisherman a courteous welcome.

'Where do you live, my friend?' he asked.

Khalifah took him to his house, where he found the lovely Kut-al-Kulub waiting. The jeweler ordered two of his servants to accompany Khalifah to a money-changer's shop, where the fisherman was rewarded with a thousand pieces of gold. When he returned, Khalifah found the jeweler mounted on a magnificent mule with all his servants gathered around him. Nearby stood another splendid mule, richly saddled and bridled, which Sheikh Kirnas invited Khalifah to ride. The fisherman, who had never been on a mule's back in all his life, at first refused, but having finally been persuaded by the merchant, he decided to risk a trial and resolutely leaped upon the animal's back – facing the wrong way and grasping its tail instead of the bridle. The mule reared, and Khalifah was thrown off to the ground to the cheers and shouts of the onlookers.

Sheikh Kirnas left the fisherman behind and rode off to the Caliph's palace. Al-Rashid was overjoyed to hear the news of his favorite's rescue and ordered the merchant to bring her immediately to his court.

The girl kissed the ground before the Caliph, and he rose and welcomed her with all his heart. Kut-al-Kulub told him the story of her adventure. Her rescuer was a fisherman called Khalifah, she said, who was now waiting at the door of the palace.

Al-Rashid sent for the fisherman, who, on entering, kissed the ground before him and humbly wished the Caliph joy.

The Caliph marveled at the fisherman's humility and politeness. He bestowed on him a generous reward: fifty thousand pieces of gold, a magnificent robe of honor, a noble mare, and slaves from the Sudan.

His audience with the Caliph over, the fisherman again kissed the ground before him and left the court a proud, rich man. As Khalifah passed through the gates of the palace, Sandal went up to him and congratulated him on his new fortune. The fisherman produced from his pocket a purse containing a thousand gold coins and offered it to the footman. But Sandal refused the gold and marveled at the man's generosity and kindness of heart.

Then Khalifah mounted the mare that Al-Rashid had given him, and, with the help of two slaves holding the bridle, rode majestically through the streets of the city until he reached his house. As he dismounted, his neighbors flocked around him inquiring about his sudden prosperity. He told them all that had happened, and they marveled at his story.

Khalifah became a frequent visitor at the court of Al-Rashid, who continued to lavish on him high dignities and favors. He bought a magnificent house and had it furnished with rare and costly objects. Then he married a beautiful, well-born maiden, and lived happily with her for the rest of his life.

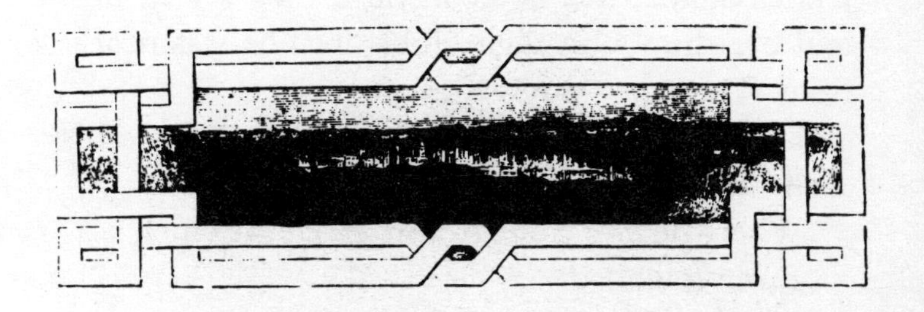

The Dream

There once lived in Baghdad a rich merchant who lost all his money by spending it unwisely. He became so poor that he could live only by doing the hardest work for very little pay.

One night he lay down to sleep with a heavy heart, and as he slept he heard a voice saying, 'Your fortune lies in Cairo. Go and seek it there.'

The very next morning he set out for Cairo and, after traveling many weeks and enduring much hardship on the way, arrived in that city. Night had fallen, and as he could not afford to stay at an inn, he lay down to sleep in the courtyard of a mosque.

Now, as chance would have it, a band of robbers entered the mosque and from there broke into an adjoining house. Awakened by the noise, the owners raised the alarm and shouted for help, whereupon the thieves made off. Presently the chief of police and his men arrived on the scene and entered the mosque. Finding the merchant from Baghdad in the courtyard, they seized him and beat him with their clubs until he was nearly dead. Then they threw him into prison.

Three days later, the chief of police ordered his men to bring the stranger before him.

'Where do you come from?' asked the chief.

'From Baghdad.'

'And what has brought you to Cairo?'

'I heard a voice in my sleep saying, "Your fortune lies in Cairo. Go and seek it there." But when I came to Cairo, the fortune I was promised proved to be the beating I received at the hands of your men.'

When he heard this, the chief of police burst out laughing. 'Know then, you fool,' he cried, 'that I, too, have heard a voice in my sleep, not just once but on three occasions. The voice said, "Go to Baghdad, and in a cobbled street lined with palm trees you will find a three-story house, with a courtyard of green marble; at the far end of the garden there is a fountain of white marble. Under the fountain a large sum of money lies buried. Go there and dig it up." But did I go? Of course not. Yet, fool that you are, you have come all the way to Cairo on the strength of a silly dream.'

Then the chief of police gave the merchant some money. 'Here,' he said, 'take this. It will help you on the way back to your own country.' From the policeman's description, the merchant realized at once that the house and garden were his own. He took the money and set out promptly on his homeward journey.

As soon as he reached his house he went into the garden, dug beneath the fountain, and uncovered a great treasure of gold and silver.

Thus the words of the dream were wondrously fulfilled, and Allah made the ruined merchant rich again.

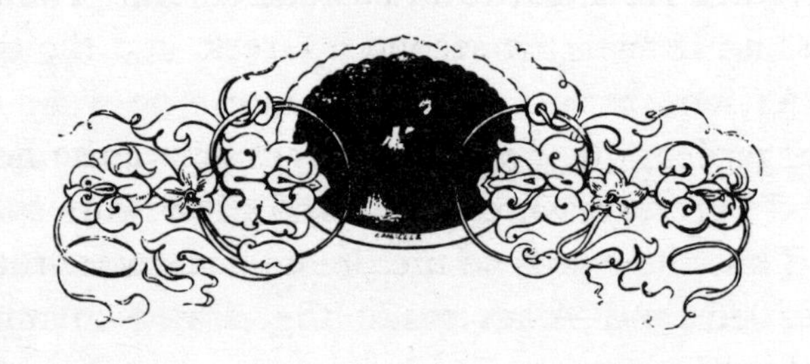

The Ebony Horse

A long time ago there lived in the land of Persia a great and powerful king named Sabur. Not only was he rich and wise, just and honorable, but he also surpassed all the rulers of his time in generosity, courage, and kindness. He had three daughters, each fairer than the full moon, and a son called Prince Kamar, who was a gallant and handsome youth.

Every year it was the King's custom to celebrate two feasts in his capital: one at the beginning of spring, and the other in the fall. During these two festivals the gates of the palace were thrown open, and alms were given to the needy and the poor. From the remotest parts of the kingdom people came to lay their presents at the King's feet.

On one of these occasions, the King was seated on his throne, surrounded by all his courtiers, when three wise men presented themselves. They were skilled in the arts and sciences and had invented many rare and curious objects. The first was an Indian, the second a Greek, and the third a Persian.

The Indian kissed the ground before the King, wished him joy, and laid before him a truly splendid gift: the golden image of a man, encrusted with precious stones and holding a golden trumpet in his hand.

'Wise Indian,' the King said, 'what is the purpose of this figure?'

'Your Majesty,' he answered, 'if you set this golden figure at the gate of your capital, he will be a guardian over it; for if your enemies march against you, he will raise the trumpet to his lips and with one shrill blast put them to flight.'

'By Allah,' the King cried, 'if what you say is true, I promise to grant you all that you desire.'

Then the Greek came forward, kissed the ground before the King, and offered him a great silver basin, which had in it a gold peacock surrounded by twenty-four gold chicks.

'Honored Greek,' said the King, 'tell us what this peacock can do.'

'Your Majesty,' he replied, 'at the stroke of

every hour of the day or night the peacock pecks one of the four and twenty chicks. Furthermore, at the end of every month, it will open its mouth and you will see the crescent moon within it.'

'By Allah,' exclaimed the King in wonderment, 'if what you say is true, you have but to name the price and it will be paid.'

Now the old Persian came forward, kissed the ground before the King, and presented him with a horse made from the blackest ebony, inlaid with gold and jewels, and harnessed with a saddle, bridle, and stirrups such as no king ever possessed. King Sabur marveled at the creature's perfection and at the excellence of the workmanship.

'Tell us what it can do,' he said.

'My lord,' the Persian answered, 'this horse will carry its rider through the air wherever he fancies, and cover a whole year's journey in a single day.'

'By Allah,' he cried to the Persian, 'if your claim proves true, I promise to fulfill your dearest wish and utmost desire.'

The wise men were entertained at the palace for three days, during which time the King put the presents to the test. He found, to his great joy, that all the claims were true: the golden image blew his gold trumpet, the gold peacock pecked its golden chicks, and the Persian mounted the ebony horse, turned a little peg near the saddle, and soared swiftly through the air, finally alighting on the very spot from which he had taken off.

'Now that I have seen these wondrous things in

action,' said the King to the wise men, 'it only remains for me to fulfill my promise. Therefore ask what you desire and it shall be granted.'

'Your Majesty,' the three answered, 'these presents are beyond all price and can be exchanged only for things of immeasurable value. Since you have given us the choice of our rewards, our request is this: your daughters' hands in marriage.'

At these words the young Prince, who was sitting his father's side, sprang to his feet.

'Father,' he cried, 'these men are old and wicked sorcerers. They are unworthy of my sisters. Surely you will never agree.'

'My son,' the King answered, 'I have given them my word, and a king's word is his bond. And just think what I can do with this wonderful horse; I *must* have it, whatever the cost. Go and ride it yourself, and then tell me what you think of the exchange.'

The Prince vaulted lightly into the saddle, thrust his feet into the stirrups, and spurred the horse on. But it did not move.

The King turned to the Persian. 'Teach my son how to ride it.'

The Persian, who had taken a dislike to the Prince because he opposed his sisters' marriage, went up to him and gave him some directions. As soon as he was shown the peg in the saddle that made the horse move, the Prince touched it and, lo! the horse flew into the air, so high and so swiftly that it was out of sight in a few moments.

When, after some hours, the Prince had not returned, King Sabur became greatly alarmed.

'Wretch,' he cried to the Persian, 'what must we do to bring him back?'

'I can do nothing, Your Majesty,' he answered. 'He gave me no time to explain the use of the second peg, and went off without learning how to come back.'

Beside himself with grief and anger, the King ordered his slaves to beat the Persian and throw him into prison; then he shut the doors of his palace and gave himself up to weeping and lamenting, together with his wife, his daughters, and his courtiers. Thus their gladness turned to sorrow and their joy to mourning.

Meanwhile the Prince had risen happily in the air until he reached the clouds and could hardly see the earth below. For a time he was thrilled with joy at the adventure, but before long he realized his danger and began to think of coming down. He turned the peg around and around, but, instead of descending, he climbed higher and higher until he feared he would strike his head against the sky.

'I am lost,' he said to himself. 'The magician must have surely meant to destroy me. And yet there must be a second peg to bring this horse to earth again. If only I could find it!'

He felt all over the horse until at last, to his great joy, he touched a very small screw on the right side of the saddle. He pressed it gently, and at once the horse slowed down. After a few moments it began to lose height as quickly as it had risen. The Prince learned how to manage the peg, the screw, and the bridle; and when he had mastered all the movements and reassured himself, he brought the horse to a comfortable height and journeyed at an easy pace, so that he could enjoy the magnificent views stretching for miles and miles below him.

Seated at his ease, the Prince flew over countries and cities he had never seen before and gazed in wonderment on all the places he passed over. When darkness fell, he found himself circling over a beautiful city that shimmered with countless golden lights, in the midst of which stood a great marble palace flanked by six high towers. He pressed the screw and guided the horse until it alighted on the roof of the palace, at the far end of which he saw a door leading to a flight of white marble steps. Leaving the ebony horse, he made his way down the steps and found himself in a marble hall, lit with lamps and candles, where a black slave lay fast asleep, guarding the entrance to a room beyond. Without a sound, he tiptoed past the slave and, drawing aside a velvet curtain, entered a richly furnished room. In the center stood a couch of ivory and alabaster studded with precious gems. Two young slave girls slept on a carpet near the door, and on the couch reclined the most beautiful girl he had ever looked upon. So beautiful was she that the Prince fell in love with her at sight and nearly fainted as he gazed at her. He approached the couch and, kneeling by her side, gently touched the girl's hand. Her eyes opened, but before she could utter a sound he begged her to be calm and fear nothing.

'Who are you, and where do you come from?' she asked in some alarm.

'I am a Prince,' he answered, 'the son of the King of Persia. It is my good fortune that has brought me to this palace, gentle lady. But if your people find me in your private room, my life will be in danger. I therefore beg you for your protection.'

The girl, who was the daughter of the King of Yemen, answered, 'Have no fear. You will be safe with me.'

She roused her slaves and ordered them to give the stranger food and drink, and to prepare a room where he might stay the night. The Prince rested and refreshed himself, and then told her of his adventure.

Princess Shams-al-Nahar (for that was her name) had never met anyone so brave and handsome as the Prince of Persia. She put on her finest robes and adorned herself with her most precious jewels, so that she might be seen in all her beauty. When the Prince came to her next morning, he was even more charmed and dazzled than before. He told her that he loved her with all his heart.

But when it was time for him to take his leave and return to his father's court, the Princess burst into tears.

'Do not cry,' he said. 'I will come back in a few days and request your hand in marriage from the King your father.'

'Take me with you,' implored the Princess. 'I cannot bear to be parted from you so soon.'

'Rise, then, and let us be off!' he cried. 'As soon as we arrive in Persia we will celebrate our marriage; then we will return in state to your father's city.'

He took the Princess up to the palace roof, sat her on the ebony horse in front of him, placed his arm tightly around her waist, and turned the magic peg. The horse rose into the air, and flew with them at great speed. Halfway through their journey, they alighted for a short rest in an orchard that was shaded with fruit trees and watered by crystal streams. After eating and refreshing themselves, they remounted the enchanted horse and flew onward to Persia. By daybreak they came in sight of King Sabur's capital, and the happy Prince brought the ebony horse to earth in the garden of his summer palace outside the city walls. He took the Princess into the palace and ordered his servants to attend her.

'I will leave you here and go tell my father, the King, of your arrival,' he said. 'Watch over my horse while I am away. I shall send messengers to bring you in state to my father's court.'

Now, when the Prince entered the city he found

the people dressed in black and everywhere saw signs of public mourning. Anxiously he hurried to his father's court.

Going up to one of the guards, he asked, 'Why is everyone in mourning?'

'The Prince! The Prince has come back!' shouted the guard. 'The Prince is alive!'

In a short while the joyful news of the Prince's return spread through the town, and the people's sorrow changed to gladness. King Sabur wept for joy on seeing him safe and sound. He embraced and kissed him, and scolded him for causing such grief and anxiety by his departure.

'Guess whom I have brought with me!' said the Prince.

'Tell me, my son.'

The Prince replied, 'I have brought to our city the daughter of the King of Yemen, the most beautiful girl in all the East.'

And the Prince proceeded to tell his father of his adventure and how he had returned home with the Princess.

'Let her be brought to our court in royal fashion,' the King cried. 'We will receive her with the utmost honor and entertain her as our guest.'

Overjoyed at his son's return, King Sabur gave orders that the Persian sage should be set free and allowed to return home. The magician, who had been expecting to suffer death at any moment, was greatly surprised at the King's pardon, and was no less bewildered by the rejoicing in the streets. Upon inquiry he was told of the return of the King's son and of the Princess who was waiting outside the city gates.

Without losing a moment, he rode off with all speed to the summer palace and, arriving there before the King's messengers, entered the hall, where he found Shams-al-Nahar lying at ease upon a couch.

'Gracious Princess,' he said, kissing the ground before her, 'the King of Persia has sent me to bring you to his court on the enchanted horse.'

The unsuspecting girl was very glad to hear this; she quickly got up and made ready to go with the supposed messenger. The Persian leaped into the saddle of the ebony horse and lifted her up behind him. When he had securely fastened her to his waist, he turned the peg and the horse rose like a bird into the air. After a few moments the Princess, to her great alarm, found she was being carried far from the city and her lover.

'Where are we going?' she cried. 'Why do you not obey your master's orders?'

'My master?' the magician echoed with an evil smile. 'Who is my master?'

'Why, the King,' she cried.

The Persian laughed.

'Do you know who I am?' he asked sharply.

'I know nothing of you except what you have told me,' answered the Princess.

'Learn, then,' said he, 'that what I told you was only a snare to trap you and the Prince. That young ruffian stole my horse from me, the work of my own hands, and the loss nearly broke my heart. Now the horse is mine again, and it is the Prince's turn to grieve. Come with me, gentle Princess, and forget that boastful youth, for I am powerful and rich, and more generous than any Prince. My slaves and servants will obey you as they obey me; I will give you jewels beyond the wealth of kings and grant your every wish and fancy.'

The Princess wept bitterly and begged the magician to take her back, but all her entreaties were of no avail. After many weary hours they reached Turkey, where the magician brought the horse to earth in a green meadow, and then went in search of food and water.

Now, this meadow was near the capital. It so happened that on that day the King of Turkey was riding nearby with his courtiers. Hearing the horses galloping past, the Princess screamed and called loudly for help. The King sent his riders to her aid and they seized the magician before he could take off on the horse. She quickly told them who she was and how she had been carried off against her will.

The King was astonished at the sorcerer's ugly appearance and the girl's extraordinary beauty. He ordered his men to throw the magician into prison, and took the Princess and the ebony horse to his own palace.

But Shams-al-Nahar's troubles were by no

means over. For no sooner had the King set eyes on her and listened to her story than he became infatuated with the Princess and resolved to marry her himself. He turned a deaf ear to her prayers and entreaties and gave orders for the wedding preparations to begin.

At last, when she saw that nothing would make him change his mind, she devised a scheme to save herself. She refused all food and drink, and began to rave and scream like a woman stricken with madness. So well did she play the part that everyone believed she was really insane. The King ordered the wedding to be postponed, and called his doctors to attend to her. But the more they saw of her, the more they were convinced that she was past all cure.

Now, all this time the Prince of Persia had been wandering with a heavy heart from land to land in search of his beloved Shams-al-Nahar, inquiring if anyone had seen or heard of a Princess and an ebony horse.

One day, at an inn in one of the great cities of Turkey, he chanced to hear the people talk about the sudden illness of a Princess who was to have married their King. He disguised himself as a doctor, went to the royal palace, and begged an audience of the King. He introduced himself as a physician long experienced in the cure of madness, and told the King he had heard of the Princess' illness and had come all the way from Persia to treat her.

'Honored doctor,' exclaimed the joyful King, 'you are most welcome.' Then he told the Prince the story of the girl's illness and all that had happened since the day he had found her with the old magician and the ebony horse.

'I have thrown the villain into prison,' he added. 'As for the horse, it is being carefully guarded in the court-yard of the palace.'

He led the Prince to the room where Shams-al-Nahar was confined. They found her weeping and tearing her clothes. The disguised Prince realized at once that her madness was not real but merely a device to avoid the marriage.

'Your Majesty,' he said, 'I must enter the room alone, or the cure will have no effect.'

The King left him, and the young man went up to the Princess and touched her hand. 'Dear Princess,' he said tenderly, 'do you not know me?'

As soon as she heard his voice she turned to him and in the great joy of recognition threw herself into his arms.

'My beloved Princess,' he said, 'be brave and patient a little longer. I have an excellent plan for our escape. But first you must make the King believe that you are improved, by talking calmly to him.'

The Prince came out of the room and said to the King, 'The girl is almost cured. Enter and speak kindly to her, and all things shall go as you wish.'

The King marveled to see so great a change in the Princess, and was overjoyed when the Prince told him he hoped she would be fully recovered by the next day. He ordered his women slaves to attend her and dress her in fine robes.

Next morning the Prince advised the King, 'Your Majesty, to complete the cure you must go with all your courtiers to the spot where you first found the Princess, and take with you the girl herself and the ebony horse. For you must know that the horse is a devil whose evil power has made her mad. I will now prepare some magic incense to break the spell that binds her; otherwise the evil spirit will once again enter her body, and our cure will work no more.'

'I will do as you wish,' the King replied, and arranged at once to leave the city for the meadow, accompanied by the Prince, the Princess, and all his retinue. When they arrived, the disguised Prince ordered the girl to sit upon the ebony horse, and placed braziers, in which a sweet incense was burning, all around her. Then, as swift as lightning, and under the gaze of all the people, he leaped onto the saddle behind the Princess and turned the peg. The horse rose straight up into the air, and in a few moments vanished from sight.

The Prince and Princess flew under the blue sky until they arrived safely in Persia. The King and all the people were overjoyed to see them after having given up hope of their return. Celebrations were held throughout the land, and they were married amid great rejoicing.

When the King died the Prince succeeded to his father's throne, and lived in happiness and peace with Shams-al-Nahar until the end of their days.

Epilogue

Night after night, for a thousand and one nights, Shahrazad told King Shahriyar strange and wondrous stories; and so charmed was he by her beauty and gentle wit that at the dawn of each day he put off her execution until the next.

Now, during this time she also bore the King three sons. On the thousand and first night, when she had ended the last of her tales, she rose and kissed the ground before him, saying, 'Great King, for a thousand and one nights I have told you stories of past ages and the legends of ancient kings. May I now make so bold as to beg a favor of Your Majesty?'

The King replied, 'Ask, and it shall be granted.'

Shahrazad called out to the nurses, saying, 'Bring me my children.'

Three little boys were instantly brought in, one walking, one crawling on all fours, and the third held in the arms of his nurse. Shahrazad ranged the little ones before the King and, again kissing the ground before him, said, 'Look upon these three whom God has granted to us. For their sake I implore you to save my life. For if you destroy the mother of these infants, they will find none among women to love them as I would.'

The King kissed his three sons, and his eyes filled with tears as he answered, 'I swear by Allah, Shahrazad, that you were already pardoned before the coming of these children. I loved you because I found you chaste and gentle, wise and eloquent. May God bless you, and bless your father and mother, your ancestors, and all your descendants. O Shahrazad, this thousand and first night is brighter for us than the day!'

Shahrazad rejoiced. She kissed the King's hand and called down blessings upon him.

The people were overjoyed at the news of the King's pardon.

Next morning Shahriyar summoned to his presence the great ones of the city, the chamberlains, the nobles, and the officers of his army. When they had all assembled in the great hall of the palace, he proclaimed his decision to spare the life of his bride. Then he called his vizier, Shahrazad's father, and invested him with a magnificent robe of honor, saying, 'God has raised up your daughter to be the savior of my people. I have found her chaste, wise, and eloquent, and repentance has come to me through her.'

Then the King gave robes of honor to the courtiers and the captains of his army, and ordered the decoration of his capital.

The city was decked and lighted; and in the streets and market squares drums were beaten, trumpets blared, and clarions sounded. The King lavished alms on the poor and the destitute, and all the people feasted at his expense for thirty days and thirty nights.

King Shahriyar reigned over his subjects in all justice, and lived happily with Shahrazad ever after.